Anonymous

Spinoza

Four Essays by Land, Kuno Fischer, J. Van Vloten, and Ernest Renan - edited by

Professor Knight

Anonymous

Spinoza
Four Essays by Land, Kuno Fischer, J. Van Vloten, and Ernest Renan - edited by Professor Knight

ISBN/EAN: 9783337294830

Printed in Europe, USA, Canada, Australia, Japan

Cover: Foto ©Andreas Hilbeck / pixelio.de

More available books at **www.hansebooks.com**

SPINOZA;

FOUR ESSAYS,

BY

LAND, KUNO FISCHER, J. VAN VLOTEN,

AND

ERNEST RENAN.

EDITED BY

PROFESSOR KNIGHT,

ST. ANDREWS.

WILLIAMS AND NORGATE,

14, HENRIETTA STREET, COVENT GARDEN, LONDON; AND
20, SOUTH FREDERICK STREET, EDINBURGH.

1882.

LONDON:
O. NORMAN AND SON, PRINTERS, HART STREET,
COVENT GARDEN.

CONTENTS.

INTRODUCTORY NOTE.

BY THE EDITOR.

My relation to this volume is a very subordinate one. I suggested its preparation, and I have revised the second Essay in the series throughout, and the others in part.

Shortly after the celebration of the bicentenary of Spinoza's death, and the unveiling of the statue in memory of him at the Hague, it occurred to me that an English version of these Essays would be a useful addition to our minor philosophical literature—the literature that is expository and critical, rather than original and creative. The appearance of Mr. Frederick Pollock's admirable work on Spinoza, and of other English monographs, has added fresh interest to the subject; while the announcement of two forthcoming books on the Dutch philosopher has extended it still further.

The Essay by Kuno Fischer—which contains an excellent summary of the life of Spinoza, and a discriminating estimate of his character—was translated some time ago by Miss Frida Schmidt, Reinwasser, Pommern. The Dutch Essays, by Land and Van Vloten—occasioned by the bicentenary celebration of the death of Spinoza, on the 21st February, 1877, and the unveiling of his statue at the Hague, on the 18th of September, 1880— were more recently translated by the Rev. Allan Menzies, of Abernyte, at present Classical Examiner to this University, who has also revised the second Essay. The fourth, by Ernest Renan, is the commemorative address delivered by him at the Hague, on the anniversary of the death of Spinoza. It was translated at the time by the late Mrs. William Smith—the widow of the author of *Thorndale*, &c.—and appeared in *The Contemporary Review*, April, 1877. The proprietors of that Review have kindly placed it at my service.

When this little work was originally projected, it was intended that it should include a lecture on "Spinoza: the Man, and his System," written for the students of Philosophy at St. Andrews, and delivered also to the Birmingham and Midland Institute, and to the Leicester, and Newcastle-on-Tyne Literary and Philosophical Societies. In that lecture, the system of Spinoza is dealt with in its relation to the doctrine of Evolution. Its publication is, however, meanwhile withheld.

At the request of Dr. Martineau—who was then engaged upon *Spinoza* for the series of "Philosophical Classics for English Readers"—I delayed the issue of this volume for some time. Dr. Martineau, however, has found it impossible to condense what he has to give us— on the life and system of Spinoza—within the limits of that Series; and the work for the "Philosophical Classics" has been undertaken by Dr. Caird, the Principal of the University of Glasgow. It seems to me that the interest in Principal Caird's forthcoming volume, and in Dr. Martineau's larger treatise, will not be lessened—but rather extended and enhanced—by the issue, in an English form, of the Dutch and German monographs, which this little book contains.

The translations of the Essays by Land and Van Vloten

have been revised by their respective authors; and Van Vloten, writing to Mr. Menzies, in August of this year, thanks him for "his happy version," which he "returns with a few unimportant suggestions." Van Vloten was the first to suggest the idea of erecting the statue, which he did in his *Benedictus de Spinoza* (1871); and a few months later a Committee was appointed to carry it out.

Professor Land has revised the translation of his Essay for this volume; and has added to it much new and important matter. His "Notes" will be found of special value. Professor Fischer and M. Renan have both taken an interest in the translation of their respective papers, but have nothing to add to their original form.

WILLIAM KNIGHT.

THE UNIVERSITY OF ST. ANDREWS,
October, 1882.

I.

IN MEMORY OF SPINOZA:

A LECTURE,

DELIVERED ON THE OCCASION OF THE BICENTENARY OF
SPINOZA, TO THE CLASS OF PHILOSOPHY AT LEYDEN,

FEBRUARY 24TH, 1877,

BY

J. LAND,

PROFESSOR OF PHILOSOPHY AT LEYDEN.

TRANSLATED BY

REV. ALLAN MENZIES,

CLASSICAL EXAMINER TO THE UNIVERSITY OF ST. ANDREWS.

PREFACE.

THE bicentenary of Spinoza's birth was not celebrated, although one of his fellow-countrymen summoned the German public to do so. That of his death was celebrated instead. A considerable gathering at the Hague, with one of the Princes of Orange at its head, listened to an *éloge* pronounced by Ernest Renan, and heard it announced by the Committee that the erection of a statue of the thinker was secured by the interest taken in the project by friends of all countries. This discharge of an old obligation—to which the indefatigable zeal of Dr. J. van Vloten provided the necessary impulse—could not be left unnoticed, in a place dedicated to the study of such thinkers as Spinoza. The following address was accordingly inserted in a course on the history of Greek Philosophy. It is an academical lecture of two hours length.

What is thus given, with the accompanying notes, makes no pretence of completeness. My object, suggested by the style of our higher instruction, was to indicate leading thoughts, historical connections, sources to be further worked out. Thus only a few citations are given from Descartes and Spinoza himself, while more is quoted from works which are difficult of access. There is still much to do for a correct knowledge of Spinoza, his precursors, his relation to the official doctrine, and to the naturalistic as well as the mystical movements of his time, and the influence he has exercised on the thought of others, down to our own times. Let the student in such fields seek to keep in view the lesson of the philosopher himself (*Tract. Pol.*, c. 1): "humanas actiones (et sermones!) non videre, non lugere, neque detestari, sed intelligere."

IN MEMORY OF SPINOZA.

A LECTURE.

To-morrow it will be two hundred years since there was laid to rest in the New Church at the Hague, the body of a private inhabitant of that town who, four days before, had died of consumption in the upper-room in which he lodged, with a single friend by his side. He was forty-four years of age, unmarried and childless, repudiated by his kindred, thrust out of the Church he belonged to, and received into no other, not even a citizen of the country in which he had been born and in which his whole life had been spent. Supported in part by a small pension which another friend had prevailed upon him to accept, he had maintained himself in his lonely dwelling by the work of his own hands, and had held intercourse only with a few. It is true that among these there were some of the foremost men of the age, who were not afraid to be seen following his funeral.

A statue is now about to be erected in honour of this man; and contributions are flowing in from the whole civilized world to aid in the design. For he was no less than our one great Dutch philosopher, Benedict de Spinoza.[1]

A university man he never was; and he declined such

1

a connection when a chair was offered to him at Heidelberg. He did not know in these days how far the freedom of philosophizing, of which he was assured when the offer was made, might be suffered to extend, without exciting the alarm of the official religion.[2] And in the Netherlands no less than in the Palatinate, regard had to be paid at that time to such considerations. Nowadays we in this country regard as an axiom the principle, which he announced and defended as a startling novelty, that the State must in its own interest leave every one at liberty to believe what seems good to him, and to state his opinions. Our higher instruction also is now in possession of that freedom—and regards it as the first condition towards the fulfilment of its task—which Spinoza could only maintain for himself at the price of remaining aloof from public life, and withdrawing his occupations as much as possible from public view. Hence there is no one to forbid us, here, to-day, in Holland's own High School, to pay our homage to the profound and noble thinker, whose works were shortly after his death strictly proscribed by the State of Holland, as "profane, atheistical, and blasphemous, on pain of the severest punishment and indignation."[3]

Spinoza was the son of one of those Portuguese Jews of Spanish descent, who, since the year 1593, had been flying in increasing numbers from the Christianity they had been compelled to profess, and the Inquisition which held its sword of Damocles suspended over them, and who, settling as foreigners at Amsterdam, enjoyed there the undisturbed exercise of their ancestral religion. He was born on the 24th of November, in the year 1632, and was brought up in the rabbinical studies, but also, in conformity with the tradition of the Pyrenæan peninsula which his friends brought with them, in the languages and the science of the West. That he might be able, were it needful, to earn his bread, he learned a trade, even at this early period of his life. Many centuries before R. Gamaliel had said: "All learning that is not accompanied with a worldly calling misses its aim and leads to perversity."[4] The work which he chose for himself was grinding optical glasses: an occupation which appears to have attracted him because it was a practical application of ascertained laws of nature, and promised him the opportunity of carrying on his own thoughts without interruption.

Most probably it was through his Latin teacher, the physician Franz van den Ende, that he was early brought into contact with the philosophy, whose praise and blame were then upon the lips of all, that of René Descartes. Yet even at this time he was no novice in the workshop of philosophy. He had already studied the writings of the most famous mediæval thinkers of his nation, and he brought with him the questions which he could hardly refrain from discussing with the freethinking physician; on whose advice he then consulted the works of the French thinker, and afterwards those of other modern writers.

The reflections of the young Israelite, fed by his reading in these two different directions, led him by degrees to peculiar results. From Jewish orthodoxy, and from the usages connected with it, he became more and more estranged. At the same time a little circle of inquirers belonging to various religious bodies, began to gather round him, and though the Cartesian system appears to have been the chief subject of their discussions, he must now and then in the course of them have given utterance

1 *

to heterodox opinions.[5] The heads of the synagogue took offence at the doctrine and the practice of the young member of their body, from whom they had formerly expected so much, and tried every means in order to retain him in their fold. When nothing was found to avail for this end, he was, before his twenty-fourth birthday, excommunicated in the most solemn manner. Both parties were true to their principles.

From this time forward he was forced to seek shelter among the Christians. He could not indeed enrol himself in a Church community, which even should it have no written creed, must always possess a standard of orthodoxy. The experience he had just undergone, and the prevailing opinions of the age, made such a step impossible. He wished to be himself, and in his search after truth to be untrammelled by any tradition. Yet he cultivated friendly relations with Mennonites and Collegiants, who like himself withdrew themselves from the authority of a meddlesome clergy. Among these people he lived for seven years : first at Ouderkerk, near Amsterdam, and then at Rhijnsburg, near Leyden, not far from that house of Endegeest, where Descartes had lived for some time. Afterwards he went to Voorburg, near the Hague, where he lodged with a simple member of the State Church ; and the last eight years of his life he spent at the Hague, in the house of people who were Lutherans. The circle of friends at Amsterdam kept up a constant communication with him : letters passed, a few visits were made on each side, and his friends studied what he sent them from time to time in writing. In addition to this he was consulted occasionally by some men of distinction and learning, such as John de Witt, Oldenburg (the secretary of the Royal Society of London), Leibnitz and Tschirnhausen, partly on subjects of natural science. He was also troubled by some persons of shallow intellect with their conscientious scruples. A journey to Utrecht, undertaken on the invitation of the Prince of Condé in the memorable year of 1673, failed in its object—the renowned general having unexpectedly departed, and being of necessity represented by some of his officers.

Apart from (1) the *Correspondence*—the last edition of which contains eighty letters, some of them from his correspondents—Spinoza's works comprise the following:

(2) A short treatise *Concerning God, and man, and his well-being.* A translation of this from the Latin has only been discovered in our days : a complete edition of it appeared in 1862. The composition of the original, which is lost to us, belongs to the Amsterdam period, or the beginning of the Ouderkerk period of Spinoza's life ; the appendix was probably written shortly before his change to Rhijnsburg.

The other works we possess, with one exception, in Latin.[6]

(3) *The Principles of the Philosophy of Descartes,* partly presented in the form of a geometrical handbook, with the addition of metaphysical reflections. This was prepared for use in the course of the instruction he gave to a young man who lived in the same house with him at Rhijnsburg, in the winter of 1662-3. It was given to the public at Amsterdam in the following summer by his friend, Dr. Lodewijk Meijer, the same who was present at his death, with an indication of important points of difference between Spinoza himself and the author he expounded.

(4) An uncompleted essay *On the Improvement of the Intellect,* belonging to the same period.

(5) The *Theologico-political Treatise,* written at Voorburg and the Hague, and edited in 1670, with all sorts of precautions to shield writer and publisher from prosecution, yet proscribed by the States.[7]

(6) *The Ethics,* Spinoza's chief work, again in geometrical form, with scholia in a more ordinary style; several times revised, and completed in 1675. Since the first treatise his views had changed in many respects; notably the mystical element which there predominates, had been forced to the background by a stricter logical sequence of thought.

(7) An uncompleted *Political Treatise,* from the last period of his life; of much less value than the theologico-political treatise.

(8) *A Hebrew Grammar,* also uncompleted, the value of which ought sooner to have been recognized.

The whole of these works—excepting the short treatise, the handbook of Cartesianism, and the theologico-political treatise—were printed by the care of Spinoza's friends from his literary remains : and as we have seen they were forthwith proscribed by the government. There afterwards appeared at the Hague, in the year 1687,

(9) *The Algebraical Calculation of the Rainbow.*

All these works are to be found collected in the Edition of Bruder, with Van Vloten's supplement. A new and cheaper, but not very accurate, edition has lately been undertaken by Dr. Hugo Ginsberg, at Leipzig.[8]

To understand Spinoza aright we must begin by placing ourselves in the circle of thought from which all his teachers set out, that of A r i s t o t l e.[9]

In everything that comes into existence Aristotle distinguishes two elements : that out of which it comes into existence, and that which it becomes; in other words "matter," and what is formed out of it. Matter *can become* what that which has form *really is*. The "potentiality" present in matter becomes "reality," by means of something else, which must be real, adding to it the form it did not possess before. What is thus formed, however, is generally capable of receiving in its turn a further form, and is contrasted accordingly as matter or potentiality with reality of a higher order, which it will attain when it undergoes a new impression, and becomes partaker of a new form. Thus we come in thought to a whole series of things to be distinguished. At the beginning, there stands in each case an abstract, pure matter, which *is* nothing, but can be made into anything; at the end, that which is entirely formed, that which *can become* nothing more, but *is really* everything. Thus, there are many degrees of perfection, or, what comes to the same thing, of reality. The Deity of Aristotle is the most perfect and the most real being. From it everything in the world borrows what it needs, in order to pass from potentiality to reality; by it everything is increasingly formed, perfected, made real. The Deity is thus also the first cause of all things.

In Aristotelianism four kinds of "causes" are distinguished. Apart from matter (causa materialis) which by itself is nothing and becomes nothing, there are the causa movens, the causa formalis and the causa finalis. Now, in virtue of His complete reality, (as actus purus) God is the first *cause of motion* (primum movens); motion signifying in this connection the transition from potentiality to reality. Again, the form of being which He bestows is a thing given in His own nature; and finally He Himself, as the *type* of perfection, is the end to

which all motion is ultimately directed. It is superfluous
here to descend to particulars. Yet we see at once that
this motion, or universal world-process, must go on from
eternity to eternity, since both matter (the moved), and
moving power, and form (the end of motion) are eternal
principles.

Here I must add that, in Aristotle, there is a certain
confusion between the cause through which a thing
exists, and the reason which obliges us to consider it as
existing. Hence, for one thing, the expression we find
even in Spinoza, that God is the cause of Himself.[10] In
Aristotelian thought this means simply that the being
(essentia) of God, defined as the most perfect and
most real being, involves His existence (existentia).
In this case, real existence seemed to be a constituent
belonging to the notion itself, though in other cases that
may not be so. And as the habit had prevailed from
Plato downwards of regarding every notion as the
representative of something that was independent and
endowed with a producing power, the existence of God
seemed actually to be founded in some way in His
essence. Not till a much later period did it come to be
seen that logical consistency gives no guarantee of the
truth of the premises we start from: that in this case
also existence cannot be the characteristic of a notion;
and that a higher stage of perfection adds nothing to
existence, which must be attributed to the full extent to
that which is lowest as well as to that which is highest.
Yet a clear view of these relations cannot be said to have
made its way everywhere in speculation even in our day.

The Jewish mediæval philosophy[11] endeavoured,
after the example of the Arabs to find unity in the materials
it received from two different sides. The theology of the

Old Testament was compared with that of Aristotle, taking the latter as the commentators of the first century of our era had mixed it up with some of the conceptions of Neo-Platonism. Jewish science could not possibly allow itself for a moment to disregard revelation ; yet it set itself the task, firstly to make it clear what an upright Jew ought to think on these subjects which the Greek thinkers laid before him for consideration, and secondly to demonstrate that the Jewish view on such subjects was also the most rational view. Among the points in question were the nature of God, his relation to the world, the freedom of man and his immortality, and the purpose of life indicated to him by his relation to his creator. Moses ben Maimun (*Maimonides*, ob. 1204) was a pure theologian, in whose eyes Aristotle was a question-putter and a teacher of method, who, wherever he came into conflict with the Bible, must give way to its authority. Yet even he did violence to the words of Scripture, now and then, by allegorical interpretation, in order to get confirmation for his doctrine. This comes out even more strongly in Levi ben Gerson (*Gersonides*) who lived a full century later, and who saw in speculation the true key to a right understanding of the sacred text, and made his way to the desired results even where his predecessor had confessed the impotence of science compared with religious faith. Proceeding on this way, there was a danger of doing more and more violence to Jewish principles and to the doctrine of the Bible, till at last nothing more was found in revelation than the doctrine of Aristotle expressed in metaphorical language which indeed was then of little use. This was seen by Chasdai Crescas, about 1400, and he came to the daring determination to give up Aristotle entirely and follow his own way within the limits of Judaism. In his work, entitled *The Light of the Word*,[12] he unhesitatingly combated the dominant system, and in so doing defended certain remarkable opinions, with which Spinoza was acquainted, as he was with those of the other Jewish scholars I have named. Of these opinions I shall mention a few.

" The unity of God's being is accompanied by a number of essential attributes which our reason must apprehend separately."

"There is neither matter, nor form, nor corporeity, that has not its orgin in God."

"What God thinks and what he wills are the same."

" God necessarily loves to impart what is good. His own being confers existence on that which His will brings with it. The creation has no end but to satisfy the demand of that love to impart what is good, which belongs to the nature of God. His blessedness also lies in such love."

" The world is a unity, in virtue of its connection with the one God, and only to this extent is it good and perfect ; while on the other side it is set together of a number of parts, and in this respect is a plurality."

" In the world everything is necessary : and the human will also is determined by its causes."

" The end of man's existence is the love of God, which is identical with the acquirement of good, and eternal communion with God's glory."

The interval between these ⌣d thinkers and Descartes was not so wide as one would imagine. Rabbi Moses ben Maimun was drawn upon by the Dominican Albertus Magnus, whose pupil, St. Thomas Aquinas, also followed him—after his own fashion—in a Summa Theologiæ.

Now we know that St. Thomas was the favourite author of Descartes from his Jesuit college days, and was almost the only theologian he had been willing to study.[13] Hence neither he nor Spinoza can be thoroughly understood by any one not acquainted with their Aristotelian antecedents, although neither of them ever read the works of the Greek thinker.

Scholasticism—how led to such a position we need not here inquire—considered that in the views of Aristotle it possessed a revelation of the true nature of things, the absolute reality independent of every appearance of it to a perceiving and thinking subject. Scholasticism applied the whole apparatus of substance, essence, causality, finality, and so on, with the same confidence with which we apply the multiplication-table; generally for the purpose of tacking on a scientific system to a received doctrine of religion; sometimes to find support for views which were not orthodox. Yet even for the orthodox this state of matters did not lead to general agreement, the Aristotelian doctrine being no more completely rounded off than the old Church doctrine, and it being possible to compel the desired agreement between the two in more ways than one. This want of unity became still more marked, when the study of the literature of antiquity gave birth to a whole world of forgotten thoughts, and the renewed pursuit of natural science began to yield its results. The violent conflict—of which the Reformation of the Church was only a part—between tradition on the one side, and the resuscitated thoughts and newly discovered truths on the other, had in the days of Descartes left on many minds an impression of general insecurity. The undisturbed conviction of a Maimonides or a Thomas Aquinas lay behind them, as a lost state of

innocence.   Then there beckoned to them a new land of
promise in mathematics, the science which had never been
driven to give up a single position, and was able to ensure
the assent of all to her assertions.   That she owed her
certitude to the nature of her subject was not yet clearly
understood.   Men sought the secret of her power in the
method of Euclid (an application, it is true, of that of
Aristotle) and deemed it possible to transfer this method
to other sciences.

Mathematics started with axioms, derived from simple
intuition.   Following the procedure of geometry,
Descartes assumed it as his first principle of method that
he should hold that to be true which presented itself to him
so clearly and evidently that it was impossible for him to
doubt it.   That which of all things could least be doubted
was for him the existence of his own *consciousness*.   This
was a masterly advance, and might have furnished the
beginning of a sound criticism of human knowledge.
Yet Descartes had retained more from scholasticism than
he himself supposed.   The " ego " to which each of us
instinctively refers his acts of sensation, thought and will,
was transformed under his hands, as if that were self-
evident, into a real thinking independent entity.   With
it there came at once, likewise by reason of its clearness
and plainness, the reality of God and of the material
world.   Here, however, he had not the same confidence
in his ground; at least he introduced an additional
guarantee in the nature of the Deity who cannot surely
mislead men.

In this way he obtained two *substances* side by side :
the thinking and the extended substance, or the spiritual
and the material.   Thought and extension were their
characteristic *attributes*, and each of these again had its

own modifications or *modi;* on the one side, for example, imagination, sensation, will; on the other, figure and motion.   Both substances derived their existence from the *concursus* of God; thus they were substances in a less thorough sense than the Creator himself.   Any action of the one upon the other (influxus physicus) was impossible, unless, again, by the divine concursus or assistance.   This action took place in man at a point in the brain, where the soul, as a being with no more of extension than a point in geometry, came in contact with the bodily organism.

The doctrine of matter or extended substance was then treated, as far as possible in conjunction with the newer physics, in accordance with mechanical principles : Descartes was himself a zealous observer of nature.   Yet here also the scholastic tradition stood in his way; as witness his failure to appreciate the significance of Galileo.[14]   Our fellow-countryman Huyghens declares at the close of the *Oosmotheoros :*[15]   This whole argument on the genesis of the comets and planets, and of the world, is constructed by Descartes out of such pointless reasonings that I often wonder how he could take so much trouble to piece together such conceits."   Competent judges declare him to have been more a mathematician than a student of Nature, though in this latter quality also he made important discoveries.

With the study of the world of mind, which he called Metaphysics, he did not occupy himself so much, though he produced a theory of the human passions.   He acknowledged, seven years before his death, that he devoted some hours every day to mathematics, and some hours every year to metaphysics.[16]   It is certain that he strove all his life to remain at peace with the authority of the Church : that at the age of twenty-nine he made a

pilgrimage to Loretto, and that the conversion of Christina
of Sweden to the Romish Church was partly attributed to
his influence.[17] Whether he practised accommodation
simply from motives of prudence, as was at one time
thought, I should be inclined to doubt, for the obvious
reason that in natural science also he was not without his
prejudices.[18]

Of other writers whom Spinoza had read I shall here
mention only G i o r d a n o B r u n o who was at first a
Dominican monk in the Neapolitan territory, but made his
escape from it, and after many wanderings was burned as
a heretic at Rome in the year 1600. He was a child of the
Italian Renaissance, and like his earlier fellow-countryman, Telesio, followed the lead of the pre-Socratic
thinkers.[19] More directly than from them, however, he
drew inspiration from Nicolaus Cusanus, a German bishop
and cardinal of the fifteenth century ; although unlike
him in being a vehement opponent of the doctrine of the
Church. He recognized only one principle, which he also
called Cause. All was in substance one, and the distinction
between form and matter disappeared as well as that
between possibility and reality. In place of a matter
which had to receive form from the outside, as ice receives
heat, he supposed a matter which brought forth all things
from its own fertile womb, an all-sufficient mother Nature,
a divinity in which were all things, and which was itself
entirely present in each thing. He distinguished this One
Being from the sum of its products or modifications : the
latter he also called the great image and only begotten
Nature : the difference consisted in this, that the universe
regarded as the sum of all things was not present in
each of its parts. At the same time the one and the
universe stood in the closest relation to each other.   In

the one infinite unchangeable there was found plurality, number. This, however, did not cause it to be multiple, but multiform—of various faces, various modi (the word which we also found in Descartes). What introduced multiplicity into things was not the essence, not the cause, but the appearance, that which announced itself to the senses, and lay on the surface of things.

As soon as he passed in thought from the highest unity to the many things in the world, he encountered two substances, a spiritual and a material; yet these might both be traced to one Being and one Root. As the perfect geometrician would be he who could reduce all the notions found in all the books of Euclid, to one comprehensive notion, so to him who should attain to perfect knowledge the multiplicity of things would be reduced to unity. In this unity he found the highest good, the highest object of desire, the source of the highest blessedness; just as we should find more delight in the unity of one precious stone, which was worth all the gold in the world, than in the plurality of millions of gold pieces, such as we might carry in our purse. This unity involved that in the world nothing could be otherwise than as it was, and that a certain cause always had a certain definite consequence. To know this unity was the final aim of all philosophy and all study of nature. A higher view, rising above Nature, was impossible except for the faithful who boasted of supernatural illumination; but such an illumination did not exist for those who sought the Deity not outside the universe, and the countless number of things, but only within them.

All these thinkers have left traces of their influence in the doctrine of Spinoza. There is scarcely an idea to be found in his writings, of which the germ at least does not occur in his predecessors. And yet we call him, and call him with reason, an original thinker. For such beings as we are, originality cannot mean that a man should produce all the elements of his work out of himself: it can only mean that he combines the elements he finds existing, in a connection they never had before, a connection which bears the stamp of his personality, and leaves unmistakable traces in the work of his successors.

To judge Spinoza fairly we must not attach too much importance to his geometrical method of demonstration. First of all, the ruling thoughts of a system of philosophy are like the conception of a work of art: the one as well as the other is prepared by all that makes the man what he is; his extraction, his surroundings, his education, his experience of life. It then appears in his consciousness in the guise of an independent power, from which he has no ability nor wish to withdraw himself, and in the service of which his reason labours to force into harmony the most obstinate facts of tradition and experience. In this way there comes into existence a system, which deserves admiration for its bold design, even where the notions employed as material and the logical masonry fail to stand the test of criticism. Nor did Spinoza consider that philosophical truth was found by the reasonings he spins before our eyes: he considered insight and intuition higher than "true reasoning," because they proceed straight to the goal without the intervention of logic.[20] The form he gave to his principal work—as he had dealt similarly before with one of the works of Descartes—had, in his eyes, a merely didactic significance. He could not count on finding in others that immediate insight, which would at once make his doctrines clear and distinct to their minds.

Comparing him with such men as Plato, Aristotle and Kant, we find in all alike the genial combination of ideas already existing, in a theory of their own, and continuous wrestlings with logic, in order to make a good rounded whole of that which from very different reasons they thought true. Viewed from without, a system of this nature always betrays certain gaps, in dealing with which logical criticism finds abundant opportunities of useful work. Thus it will always be till the time comes when the perfect system is discovered. But then also the age of inquiry will have had an end for evermore, and eternal truth reign on earth without a rival.

Spinoza himself tells us by what road he came to philosophical inquiry.[21] He had found that all those things which men generally seek after, riches, honour, pleasure, do not permanently satisfy. He asked if it were possible to discover and acquire that by means of which he would partake of perfect and enduring happiness. Nothing, he saw, but love to the eternal and infinite could bestow on him this joy. The highest good consisted for him in this that he himself, and as many others as possible by his means, should come to the knowledge of " that unity which connects the mind of man with the whole of nature."

Hence he sought to understand so much of nature as was necessary in order to arrive at this knowledge. It was quite otherwise with Descartes, who demanded from science first of all a firm foundation for his mathematico-physical investigations, and in other matters contented himself with the chief doctrines of a moderate Catholicism. With Spinoza what stands in the forefront is the ethical need of a cheerful view of life, a need, however, which he felt could only be satisfied through the insight acquired by reason into the nature of existing things. He thus presumed, even before the outset of his inquiry, that the nature of things, once known according to its truth, would justify an optimistic interpretation. This presumption was to him an object of unconditional belief; and he, who attaches a higher value to the faith of the heart than to a well-arranged dogmatic, must at once feel reverence for the man who drew from this source the courage he required, to defend as life-quickening truth—and to maintain consistently to his death—a doctrine which to the eyes of most men appeared to be heartless and comfortless.

At the head of this doctrine there stands a notion of God which is quite peculiar. The theologies which appeal to the Bible constantly alternate between the idea of a Being of exalted human qualities, who made the world at a certain time and continues to uphold it, and that of a Being to be compared with nothing else, without whom the world could not exist, but who at the same time would not exist without a world. Such questions as these: From what can the world be made, if not from a principle that was present in God Himself? and what could necessitate Him to begin at a certain time the work of creation?—drive theology back from the popular mythical idea: and the recognition of the reality of pain and evil, even more than the words of Scripture, make it impossible for her to accept the complete unity of essence of God and the world.[22] Spinoza denies the reality of these apparent disturbances, and is thus enabled to hold the immanence of God in the world, with all the consequences of that position. With him, as with Bruno, the two are not simply identified; he distinguishes the one principle from the sum of things, or to borrow an expression of certain nameless Thomists, *natura naturans* from *natura naturata*.[23] God, the infinite and perfect being, has Himself an infinite number of attributes; of these thought and extension are two, and the only ones known to us. The two independent substances of Descartes are thus in this system made one in the divine substance; the characteristic attributes of both are ascribed to the Deity, and in addition to these an infinite number of others which we do not know.[24] This last step was necessary, as otherwise the infiniteness of the Divine Being might seem to be compromised; and here we have a second indication that the Deity of Spinoza is not to be confounded with the world, the world of our knowledge being nothing more than the modi of two of the attributes.

Descartes had declared that all things were created by the good pleasure of God, and that the reason why the three angles of a triangle were equal to two right angles was that God had so willed it. Spinoza refuses to allow that God could forbear to do what He does. That which brings Him to do anything can be nothing but His own perfection; and His freedom consists simply in this, that He cannot be forced to anything from without, because there is nothing outside of Him. Here Spinoza is at one with Crescas against Maimonides. But he goes even further than Crescas, who, as a believing Jew, had always spoken of God's will.[25] With Bruno Nature resembled an animal organism, being individual and yet furnished with a multiplicity of organs and manifestations of life. We shall best understand Spinoza if we suppose that what was before his mind was the relation between a datum of mathematics and what is necessarily connected with it.

I have already pointed to the fact that from certain

passages of Aristotle a confusion had arisen between the
cause and the reason, the real condition of existence and
the logical premiss.   Hence, for instance, the expression
in Descartes that the infiniteness of God's nature is the
"cause or reason" why he requires no "cause" for his
own existence.   Neither the one word nor the other
satisfies him, and he therefore uses both.   The same is
true of Spinoza where he speaks of "cause" and also
where he speaks of "reason or cause."   He seeks for a
common word, mindful of his principle to speak in such
a way that common people will understand him[26]—and
he fails to find it, the reason being that he has something
new to say, for which there is no name in common use,
and that he has not yet given himself a clear account of
this new idea.[27]   Geometry supplies him with the notion
he is in search of.   In a triangle having its angles equal
the sides are also equal.   The equality of the sides is not
produced by that of the angles as a cause; for then the
angles must have existed before the sides.   As little is
it a sufficient account of the relation to say that the
equality of the angles is the reason why we must hold
the sides to be equal.   No, the first equality is a reason
to us only on the ground that in the triangle it is something more than that equality; a thing that cannot be
there without the other equality being there as well.
Thus what we find here is akin both to the cause and to
the reason; but it is not to be confounded with either.
It is not present sooner than that which may be said to
proceed from it; and the relation between the two is
different from a merely logical one.   In the same way
God with Spinoza is not present before the world, which
is indeed as eternal as He: and as little is the relation
between the two such, that his existence makes that of

the world a logical necessity. His existence is as necessarily connected with the existence of the world as it is, as the existence of the three equal angles of a triangle is necessarily connected with that of its three equal sides, or the existence of a circle with that of a hundred relations between magnitudes of which geometry gives us the account. Our understanding comes after and proves the equality of the sides or the relations one by one, by regarding and drawing consequences from the supposition of equal angles or of a circle, the construction of which in our imagination is set forth by its definition.[28] Similarly, our philosopher seeks by a demonstration—after the manner of geometry—to deduce his doctrine of the world from his definition of God, as the substance with infinite attributes, two of which are thought and extension; he means that the doctrine follows by necessity from the supposition of a Being thus defined. He imagines that, to the relation which exists for the reason between the fact before it and the deduction therefrom, there corresponds a real relation between the circle and the proportion connected with it, or between God and the world which depends on him. Hence, the word Cause, as applied to him, and the expression that—from the necessity of the divine nature—infinite things must follow in an infinite manner. To bring his thought to full clearness, Spinoza should have gone a step further. God and the world are to him correlates, as much as the equality of the angles and that of the sides, as much as the circle and the relations of magnitudes connected with it. It is possible in geometry to deduce the second from the first: but the first may equally well be deduced from the second. The word Cause is not a fit one in this part of the system: if it is to be used, the world may

with equal correctness be called the cause of God. If
we let the word go, with the whole logical apparatus
connected with it, and hold fast simply the mathematical
analogy, the conception of Spinoza will appear in clear
daylight.

It is a conception on which no one had ventured
before him. Parmenides, it is true, taught the unity of
all being; but he had no account to give of the world of
things, a world of appearance, woven together of being
and not-being. Heraclitus found in all things the successive changes of the ever-living fire; but the fire itself
was always going out, and always kindling: a constant
becoming rather than a constant being. The Stoa,
which in other respects frequently reminds us of Spinoza,
and which was deeply indebted to Heraclitus, knew only
of an indissoluble connection between two eternal principles, the active Deity and passive matter. With our
thinker the one substance is real, and equally real are its
attributes and its modi. That it is the same from eternity
to eternity, and that things arise and pass away according
to a fixed order, is equally an essential part of its nature.

We ought not to compare Spinoza with those who,
from superficiality, or in consequence of critical investigation, renounce the problem of absolute being, but with
those who seek to solve it. And then we see that all
who are enlisted on this side assert in one way or another
the essential unity of things which are in appearance
conflicting; and we do not see that with our means any
other course is possible. Every metaphysic which aims
at being a theory of the absolutely real, is, so far as we
can see, an impossible metaphysic; sooner or later its
logical weakness will become manifest. Hence one theory
succeeds another, and this must go on till either we have

learned to avoid all logical difficulties, or come to see that in such a product of the mind these difficulties are unavoidable. Spinoza has this merit above many, that he takes the difficulty of thinking unity together with plurality, persistency with changeableness, for what it is, and attributes the one and the other alike to the constitution of things. Thus he relieves himself of the hopeless task of making the one proceed out of the other; the attributes out of the substance, or the modi out of the attributes; and escapes all disputes about creation, emanation, and cosmogony in general. He feels that the relation we have to do with here is of a peculiar nature, which cannot be compared with a relation between things in the world, such as that between maker and made, mother and child, flame and ray. Only the relation between geometrical facts may in some measure illustrate it. The world of the modi, in which everything changes after the order of time, has for its reverse the eternal, *i.e.* here, the timeless Being of the one substance.[20] Though this fundamental thought is still developed in scholastic forms, which fit it but clumsily, yet it prevents the occurrence of a multitude of scholastic questions.

The novelty of this thought makes it impracticable to assign to it a place in any of the customary pigeon-holes. Those who have made the attempt have evidently found it a perplexing one. Most have considered, as the States of Holland did in his own time, with their spiritual counsellors, that Spinoza must be an "atheist." Others, on the contrary, asserted that with him everything was taken up into the Deity, so that, like Parmenides, he had no world remaining, and must be called an "acosmist." Others, again, had remarked that he raised the universe to a Deity, and called him a "monistic pantheist."

Some one finally discovered that he had announced the unity of substance only for the sake of the uninitiated public, and that his own conviction must be characterized as atomistic-automatic pantheism.[30]   There is something to be said for each of these designations: but if our object is to understand the man, the better plan will be simply to call him Spinoza, and to learn from himself what he had sought and what he had found.

As was to be expected, the successive states in Spinoza's world are ruled by the strictest *causal nexus*. No finite thing, no "modus" can exist or act, unless determined to existence or action by some other finite thing.   There is nothing that could be other than it is, nor does the determination of the human will constitute any exception to this.   Along with this we are told that everything is determined by the necessity of the divine nature, and that God is the cause of things.   How does the one assertion agree with the other?   A current of air at a certain low temperature strikes the surface of a sheet of water: the fact described in these words is a sufficient cause for the appearance of a sheet of ice on the water.   Were anything wanting in the conditions which we comprise in this statement of the fact, the ice would not appear.   But there is something else of which we must take account: the law of nature according to which the conditions described necessarily lead to the appearance of ice.   It also, if we choose, may be called the Cause of the sheet of ice; but in another sense, be it remarked, than the fact already described.   The fact, moreover, is one link in the chain of real events which occurs at a certain time, although something of the same kind is observed to take place in every similar occurrence.   The law of nature, on the contrary, we represent to ourselves as eternally existing, being founded in the nature of water, of air, and of heat, and equally valid even were, for example, the chemical elements distributed in such a way in space that the occurrence never took place in reality, and the sheet of ice never came into existence. "Law of nature" is a metaphorical expression.[31] If we regard that which we understand by it as a necessity, based in the nature of things, or in Spinozistic phrase, in the divine nature, then the matter grows plain to us. That B may appear, or come into operation, there is needed not only A, but also the necessity based in the nature of A and B, by which B is connected with A.

At this point, however, a sharp distinction is drawn, with Descartes, between the modi of the one and those of the other attribute. The modi of each attribute have God for their cause, only in so far as he is regarded under that attribute of which they are the modi. In other words, material nature is exclusively subject to physical laws, and conscious life only to psychological laws. The body brings about no thoughts or affections in the mind, and the mind produces no motions in the body. Here the road is opened to modern mechanical natural science, which we indeed can follow more thoroughly than was possible to Spinoza. Yet the most intimate connection exists between the two kinds of modi. Not only is the order of thoughts entirely the same with the order of external things, but that which exists in space on the one hand, and the clear and perfect idea of it in the mind on the other, are the same thing, expressed in two different ways, or seen from two different sides.[32]

The human mind is nothing but the clear and perfect idea of the human body, and is thus so far one with the body. This body exists in time, and consists of many parts, each with a number of subordinate parts; it is affected in many ways by other bodies and acts on them in turn, also in many ways. And the states of the body are in all respects *parallel* to those of the mind. Our mind, however, is the idea of the body, not as it is in itself, but as it is in respect of its states; hence it knows itself in no other way than as a succession of bodily states.[33] Thus the elevation of the empirical ego to a substantial individual soul. is not guaranteed by consciousness, as with Descartes. The conscious subject finds in itself nothing but a succession of ideas, which refer to none but bodily states. Those who are conversant with the works of modern psychologists, such as Bain and Wundt, will recognize the modern character of Spinoza's doctrine on this point.[34]

As, however, the states of the body are changed from without, the idea of them is constantly accompanied by that of external things putting forth influence. But the knowledge which is gained in this way by chance encounters, *i.e.* by a rough empirical process, is confused and unsatisfactory. It requires to be completed by comparison, through which we rise to general ideas. As it is expressed in the school terms of our own day, the laws of nature are discovered by induction from particular observations. Yet what is obtained in this way must with Spinoza still yield to the intuitive knowledge, conceived after the analogy of mathematical knowledge, which is based on the correct idea of the true nature of some of God's attributes. Empirical knowledge Spinoza calls "belief;" that which is intuitive is with him "clear knowledge," an apodeictic knowledge as compared with the knowledge made up of assertions, to which experience leads us. With this thinker there is no doubt that he sees that which is real face to face. "How," he says, "is any one to know that he understands a thing, unless he actually understands it? As light manifests itself and darkness as well, so the truth is the test of itself and of untruth too." [35]

In studying any strictly monistic system we are confronted with the question; if everything in the world is bound to a fixed order, and if human thought forms no exception to this, whence, in so well-ordered a universe, comes the possibility of error and of false appearance? Spinoza's answer to this is that all ideas are true so far as they are all present in God; and none of them is untrue, save in so far as it is referred to the human mind. For his dogmatic age this is an uncommonly subtle remark, though still wrestling with the trammels of the scholastic tradition. In fact from the standpoint of pure determinism every idea must be regarded as being just what it must be of necessity, under the given conditions and subject to the natural laws of thought. Here the distinction between true and untrue does not occur: from this point of view there are no untrue ideas. Spinoza saw this perfectly: even he might have felt it necessary to add, as little from such a point of view can we speak of true ideas. The distinction appears only when we regard the idea as satisfying or failing to satisfy the claims which man, occupying the position of a logical being, must put forward. That this is the only possible standpoint for us, Geulinx[36] alone in those days appears to have surmised. Spinoza, firmly convinced, like many others, that he possessed a knowledge of the absolute being, saw very well that at a high standpoint, such as he held himself to occupy, all untruth resolved itself into

mere one-sided view, which under certain circumstances
was no more than natural.

Where the mind does not act on the material world,
the will, too, cannot be what is generally understood by
the name. Even with Descartes the will had become a
"power to judge and to choose." To pass over into
action it required the divine assistance; yet it was clear
and distinctly obvious, *i.e.* no one thought of doubting,
that there is found in us men freedom and indifference.
In the ethics of our thinker this faculty disappears
entirely. Nothing remains of it but particular deter-
minations of the will, which contain no more than the
affirmation or denial that such and such a thing is good.
Thus the will falls under the higher notion of the reason.
" I will this," signifies simply, "I think this good," or,
what is the same thing, "I think this useful for me."
This judgment, like everything else in the world, is
determined by an infinite series of causes; and the
proximate cause of our choice, *i.e.* the centre of the will,
is our striving towards the object, not, as with Descartes,
our choice the cause of our striving. This striving is
identical with the constant impulse, residing in the nature
of each thing, to persist in its own being. Actual
existence and unlimited self-assertion are always found
together, and every disturbing or destroying influence
must necessarily come from without.[37]

Thus we come to the Spinozistic doctrine of the
emotions, among which the passions are included. They
all arise from desire, pleasure, and pain — the three
primary emotions. Desire is the natural striving after
self-preservation of unlimited duration, in so far as such
striving is thought in connection with both mind and
body. Pleasure and pain are states to produce which

something outside of ourselves co-operates, and by which
the power of the mind for thought, or, what is the same
thing, its perfection or reality is exalted or lowered.
Mind and body are so intimately connected that each
affection of the mind has its counterpart in the body.
That which in reference to the mind alone was called
will, is in reference to both sides of human existence
called desire. In the same way pleasure is connected
with good spirits, pain with low spirits. Thus each
emotion must be called a state of the body as well as
of the mind. Here we have the basis of a natural
history of character which, up to the present day, has
been replaced by no better. Love and hatred, for
example, are pleasure and pain in connection with the
idea of an outward cause: hence comes the desire to
have and keep the object of this idea with ourselves, or
on the other hand to remove and destroy it. This,
however, does not make man an egoist by nature; it is
enough that we imagine a being like ourselves, though
on other accounts indifferent to us, and we shall ourselves
feel the pleasure or pain we ascribe to that being, and
shall love or hate the causes of that pleasure or pain.
Hence comes what we do for the sake of our fellow-men ;
and, according to circumstances, our self-satisfaction or
our repentance. Hence also it comes that the views of
others have power to strengthen us, or to make us waver
in our inclinations and aversions. For the same reason
we seek to be loved in return, and are proud of that
when it takes place. On the other side, however, human
life is not purely idyllic. Strife and jealousy arise where
only one person can enjoy the object of our love. In
certain circumstances love can pass over into hatred, and
the hatred will be the more intense, the warmer the love

has been. The converse of this can also take place. All this depends partly on the constitution of the individual, partly on the circumstances in which he may find himself at the time, and partly on the objects which fill us with pleasure or pain. The thing follows its regular course, like every other part of nature. "By outward causes we are driven hither and thither, as the billows of the sea by conflicting winds, and know not what is to become of us." A distinction between good and evil is never even spoken of in this connection; our thinker keeps the notion good even more strictly at a distance from his view of the absolute essence of things than the notion true. How can such a notion find any application to dispositions or to actions which are regarded solely as the inevitable consequences of what went before them?

Yet here also there is another side to which we must attend. The states of mind are all on one level, in so far as they constitute a part of the whole sum of things, and are all alike subject to the law of cause and effect. Yet they are at the same time the states of a human individual, and with regard to his welfare they are *advantageous* or *hurtful*. Each one must desire that those states which are advantageous shall fall to his lot as much, and those which are hurtful as little, as possible. Now we might readily suppose that, in a world like that of Spinoza, such a wish must be vain : that indeed no one can withdraw himself from the blind sport of outward influences which introduce change into his lot without consulting his interests. Our thinker has given up the Deity outside the world which cares like a mother for her children. Nor is that comfort available for him which makes his predestination endurable to the Calvinist, the comfort namely of thinking that all has been ordained as it is by the highest wisdom and goodness. What rules with him is *necessity*, the nature of things; and here another stigma awaits him : he is called a "fatalist." [38] When we hear of a fatalist, we at once think of a Turk, who makes up his mind to the inevitable, and takes good care not to be led by any ideal he has formed to interfere in the course of events. Spinoza is of a very different mind from this. With him necessity is no blind fate, to which God and men are subject as to a foreign power, but it is the true nature of ourselves and of surrounding things. He will not have us submit to necessity as we do to circumstances outside of ourselves ; he will have us understand it, as identical with our own nature, and by becoming reconciled in our mind with the order of the universe find peace with ourselves. Nor is the inward peace all that is thus brought about. In the right understanding of the universal order, Spinoza finds the motive and the standard of an activity such as befits the reasonable man. He who is called a fatalist undertakes to point out to the more highly gifted the way to freedom, and with respect to the great multitude to define the constitution of society by which they will approach to freedom most nearly, and by which the upward path will be opened for them as widely as possible. The first he seeks to do in the last books of the Ethics : the second in the Theologico-political Treatise:

Human freedom is, with Spinoza, not the absence of determination, not indifference—as with Descartes—but it is of the same nature as the freedom we saw him attribute to the Deity ; the being determined not from without, but by a man's own nature, by the law that is in him. What that law is reason teaches us, and freedom is therefore

identical with obedience to reason. Reason requires of
us that each man should seek his own true advantage,
and desire all that truly leads him upwards to perfection;
in other words, that each man should endeavour to
preserve his own being, so far as in him lies. The more
he does this, the greater is his *virtue:* the first and only
foundation of virtue is self-preservation. This has been
interpreted as egoism. Some have pointed out, with a
pleasurable regret, how little this Jew was penetrated
with the exalted idea of Christian love. They forgot,
however, that what is in question here is not temporal
advantages, but eternal welfare; and that no Christian
love has ever held it lawful for a man to give up his own
part in paradise for the sake of another. Only such an
injunction as this could be contrasted with that of
Spinoza's *Ethics.* He never for a moment conceives that
one man's true advantage could be attained at the expense
of that of another: on the contrary, he is convinced that
when each man seeks that which is truly useful to him,
men will render the best service to each other. The
highest good for those who seek after virtue—the knowledge of God—is common to all, and all may enjoy it
alike. Those who are seeking this desire the good they
seek, not only for themselves, but for other men as well;
and this the more, the further they have advanced in the
knowledge of God. Knowledge, I said, is for the mind
the highest good; and it is at the same time the highest
virtue. What the mind seeks is certainly to live, to
preserve itself, to determine itself out of its own nature,
i.e., to act instead of to suffer. Now the acting of the
mind is knowing, its perfection consists in perfect knowledge, and all things are truly known, only when they
are known in their connection with the highest Being.

If we let reason guide us, we shall consider whatever promotes *the life of men together,* as useful or good ; we shall consider whatever brings discord into society, as evil. Hatred is a sort of pain, and no sensible man would willingly take upon himself such an evil. In addition to this, it is contrary to the general interest, and each man ought for his own sake to contend with it. The only effective weapons against hatred, anger, and scorn, are love and generosity. The hostile attitude another takes up towards us can rest on nothing but misunderstanding. If it be possible to remove the misunderstanding, by raising up the whole man to a higher stage of development, so much the better : but, in the first instance, in our relations with man in general, we must recognize the principle that an emotion of the mind can only be overcome by a stronger emotion. And though the love with which we meet our enemy may sometimes be misconstrued, and our aim in a particular case disappointed, yet we bow willingly before the superior force. We do so from a clear conviction, and accordingly from an increase, not a decrease, of our own power. The wisest man feels it no humiliation that now and then he must be content to go to the wall.

That this system of Ethics was not borrowed, as has been asserted, from one or another form of Christianity,[39] is clear from the estimate given of such states as pity, humility, and repentance. Pity is pain, and thus an evil ; humility, the contemplation of our own impotence, our limitation by the external world, unnerves our spirit ; repentance, vexation at an accomplished fact for which we consider ourselves responsible, robs us of the self-confidence we need for the future. Here, however, let me at once add, our thinker has in his eye only the man

who lives according to reason. He calls it inhuman, if a
man does not suffer himself to be moved either by reason
or by pity to come to the assistance of others : he sees
that that pride—that boundless self-confidence, which
makes the unenlightened man the shameless slave of his
passions—must be broken, before truth can enter into
him. In a certain sense, at a certain stage, that may be
virtue, or rather may lead to virtue, which at the highest
standpoint, for the man living according to reason,
becomes a sign of imperfection. Who would not rather
be treated in a dangerous illness by a strange physician,
in the full possession of his art, because to him the
sufferer is simply an object for the careful application of
his skill, than by an equally able friend whose medical
eye might be obscured by the tears of sympathy ? Those
sisters of charity are not the least useful who are not so
much troubled with the misery they have to deal with as
anxious to earn heaven for themselves. Be it remarked
that what is spoken of here is not love but pity. Love
to one's neighbour is, according to Spinoza, perfectly
rational. The reasonable man naturally desires that the
good he wishes for himself should be shared by others
as well. He has an interest in the virtuous acting he
witnesses in others, and is favourably disposed to them
personally on account of it. Their approbation is welcome to him, and he is most closely connected by the ties
of friendship and gratitude with all right-thinking men.
It is true that he withdraws himself, so far as possible,
from the benefits of the unenlightened. But why does
he do this ? Because the benefits, which they think in
their ignorance they are conferring upon him, are really
a hindrance to him in his upward way. They know not
how to serve him, and yet they would be disappointed if

they learned how little importance he attaches to things which they think desirable for all. In order not to hurt their feelings he will arrange when he can to avoid their officiousness.

In fact, what Spinoza means by his self-preservation is not egoism but autonomy; not self-seeking, but the privilege of self-realization. This privilege, this freedom, the condition of sanctification for a thinker, he expects to attain precisely by means of insight into the absolute necessity of all things, as they are based in the unalterable nature of Being, in the nature of the Deity. Things must be looked at, as he expresses it, with an eye to their eternal significance, " *sub quadam æternitatis specie.*" Then it appears that all pain and evil exist not absolutely, but only in reference to some particular modus of the absolute Being. Then the emotions lose their power, since hatred, anger, jealousy, scorn, arrogance, and so on, are based simply on a confused and imperfect view of what exists. Only the effort after perfection, and love to our neighbour are left to us. The object of our aspiration then ceases to be to escape from a perverted world by death, and migrate to a better, according to the saying which has been repeated ever since Plato, that philosophy is a meditation on death;[40] it is rather to find our place in the world, to rise superior to apparent pain and evil by the increase of our knowledge in every direction, and to make our philosophy a meditation on life. Then we are free, because we live according to our well-understood nature. And in this freedom we find our *salvation.* For, as we know ourselves as we are in ourselves—not as we are limited and hindered from with-, out—our strength receives increase, we pass on to higher perfection, or, what is the same thing, we are filled with joy. This is the joy which goes hand in hand with the idea of God, to whom we have learned to refer all things, and is thus the same as *love to God.* This love to God is an altogether peculiar thing. The loved object is itself incapable of all emotion, and loves no one as it hates no one, so that here it would be folly to ask for a returning love. Our feeling for the Deity can only be strengthened by others taking part in it. It is an intellectual love, without jealousy, without blindness, without disappointment, without passion. It is related to love for a worldly object, as the eternal is related to that which exists in time. It is our eternal nature which is concerned with it, and it is therefore not different from the love with which God loves himself, in so far at least as this love resides in that one of his modi which we call the human spirit. The " Ethics " thus issues in the mystical identification of self with the Deity, in which thousands, from India to Northern Europe, have found peace. Immortality is a necessary feature of such a position ; but with Spinoza it is not a continuance in time, but an existence outside of time, in which the individual existence loses its preponderating significance. Of this we find the first suggestion even in Plato and Aristotle.[41] The expression, " The mind is not destroyed with the body, but something of it survives eternally," sounds like a concession to prevailing opinion. He adds expressly that, although we know nothing of the eternity of our mind, we ought nevertheless to place before ourselves the same aim of life, since it is the only natural and rational one for us. But salvation is not the reward that we receive because we took upon ourselves the burden of virtue; it is virtue, it is excellence itself. It has nothing to do with what happens to us. It dwells in us, where and when we are in fellowship of spirit with the eternal Being, with whom indeed we stand in the closest communion even by nature.

Yet only to few is it allowed to rise above the tumult of the passions into the blessed calm of the life of reason. As for the multitude who are incapable of philosophic thought, and therefore devoid of the true knowledge of God, are they to be left to their fate ? Spinoza did not forget the multitude. Man can be saved, even when he does not understand the eternal law or the law of reason, simply by obeying it. The law, so far as man needs it for his salvation, is laid down in the form of Divine commandments, in the Jewish and Christian Scriptures ; and the State—erected and maintained by men to meet their need of concord and mutual assistance—best answers its natural purpose, when it is regulated and governed in the spirit of the morality of the Bible. Here, however, everything depends on the manner in which the Bible is read, that its true teaching may be drawn from it. The Theologico-political Treatise contains accordingly the principles of hermeneutics and those of politics connected together in one work.[42]

Our thinker has long been recognized as one of the precursors of the modern study of the Bible. In studying the Bible he would have grammar regarded as the foundation, and first of all Hebrew grammar, since the writers of the New Testament, as well as those of the Old, were Jews. Each text must be interpreted in its own historical connection, the doctrine of each writer must be gathered from his own words viewed by themselves, and not mixed up either with that of the other writers or with the particular opinions of the expounder and his contemporaries. The history of each book must be traced, we must ask about the person of the author, the circumstances in which the book was written; its further fortunes, and its reception into the canon. To this is to be added the inquiry as to the purity of the text. Spinoza understands perfectly that the difficulties, with which the expounder has to contend, proceed in great part from the fact that so few manuscripts have been preserved, and from the peculiarities of Hebrew style and writing. He expects no help from supernatural light, nor from the authority of any Church, nor from philosophical views, but only from historical investigation. He sees no essential difference between a belief in miracles and ignorance. Miracle is not what is incomprehensible yet actual, but rather what fills the multitude with astonishment: for, he says with reason, the multitude considers that it sufficiently understands a thing only when it no longer wonders at it, though for no other reason than that it has grown familiar. Many miraculous narratives are intelligible enough to the inquirer who regards them as composed in a spirit of self-glorification, to show the special favour of the Deity enjoyed by the writer and his companions, *i.e.*, to exhibit them as the central point of nature.

It lies outside of our purpose to discuss the remarkable contributions of Spinoza to what is called the Introduction to the Bible, and to historical Criticism. It is only in our own century that the true significance of these has been recognized. It is of more importance to us to remark that he places the value of the Bible in its being a means of instruction for the people. The aim of the sacred writers is not to make the people learned, nor philosophically enlightened, but obedient, upright and compassionate, and religiously disposed—even when unable to attain to the true knowledge of God, which is the fruit of the highest thought alone. He would have religion and philosophy kept separate, and not brought into the arena either with or against each other, inasmuch as they are not intended for the same individuals, though both leading to salvation, each in its own way.

The religion of the Bible, made known by thorough exegesis, is thus of the highest value for the non-philosophical individual. *Society* owes to it the possibility of rational improvement. On the subject of society, Spinoza follows for the most part the doctrine of his older contemporary, Thomas Hobbes.[43] Everyone has by nature a right to exist, and to make himself master of all that can be profitable to him. If all lived in accordance with reason, then their interests would be in harmony, since all would desire the one highest good for themselves and for each other. Blinded, however, by ignorance, they seek their advantage in opposite directions, and come in conflict with each other. In this state of matters the only means to secure concord and mutual assistance is to form an agreement in virtue of which each surrenders something of his right, and all join in guaranteeing to each the undisturbed enjoyment of what is left after this surrender. Spinoza does not propose to trace the road, by which the growth and the modification of society has come about, in course of time ; his aim is simply to explain what society is, in the view of the thoughtful citizen. Such a one feels himself morally bound to society, not because it can prove a supernatural right, nor merely because he was born in it ; but because he approves of it, as the state which enables him, and all others, to pursue their true interest with the least possible interference. The right and title of society, whatever be its historical genesis, is before the tribunal of reason nothing but the consent of all sensible people. The community, resting on this as its basis, is entitled to give laws, and inflict punishments; and obedience or resistance to its behests is to be recognized thereafter as that which is right or wrong. Society alone retains a full natural right to all that can be for its advantage. Spinoza could not take for granted any law of nations, anterior to treaties formed between societies or states: societies possess every possible right to wage war on each other, to rob each other, to reduce each other to subjection.   When this principle, however, is carried out to its ultimate results, it is found that, in this case also, the permanent advantage of all requires that the state of lawlessness should be brought to an end, and war with all that it involves removed from the world by international agreements.   In politics, as in ethics, our philosopher is a utilitarian, if any one cares to insist on the name: yet let it not be forgotten that he is not content with welfare and prosperity, but subordinates everything to the perfecting of man as a reasonable being.   His self-preservation is quite a different thing from the " preservation of life and limb" of Hobbes.   If he asks for unconditional obedience to the laws of the state—a demand which every state not yet effete puts forward habitually and vigorously—he is not thinking of any tyranny that may occur to us, but of the well-constituted commonwealth, or what under any given circumstances is the nearest approach to it.   The ideal of Hobbes was an absolute monarchy (which he makes equivalent to a tyranny), provided it were either originated or confirmed by the will of the people, like the Bonapartist Empire with its plebiscites.   He gathered up all power in the person of the sovereign, to such an extent as to render impossible the publication of opinions not

officially sanctioned. Whether any particular doctrine
was religion or superstition depended with him simply on
the decision of the sovereign; whether it was the true
religion, on the orthodoxy of the sovereign, as he might
explain it. The mysteries of the faith were to be accepted
without proof and without further definition, as we
swallow a pill which is prescribed for us without chewing
or tasting it. Prescribed is here the proper word:
submission to Holy Scripture was based on submission to
the Church; and the Church was identical with the Christian
state, that is, once more, the sovereign, the pope-king.
Spinoza, on the contrary, in the single passage in which
he mentions Hobbes, lays stress on the fact, that in his
own state the original right of the citizen is not lost, but
only conjoined with that of his fellow-citizens to form an
organic whole. He demands no submission to the state
as a superior being, but simply recognition of its power
over the individual, and of its indispensableness. Although
denying the independence of the modus as against the
substance, he is maintaining that of the individual man
as against society. The being of the modus is based on
that of the substance; the being of the state on the
contrary is based on that of the citizen who institutes and
upholds it. The state has to reckon with the natural
limits of its power. For the magistrate the maintenance
of his power depends in the first place on the good faith
of the citizens, and then on the promptitude and resolution
with which the laws are put in force. That magistrate is
in the fullest sense master of his subjects who knows how
to be master of their dispositions. And therefore, while
public worship must remain within the limits assigned to
it in the interests of good order—and it is for the advan-

tage of religion and piety itself that this should be the case—the state must for its own sake concede full liberty of thought and speech.

Thus, not only has the state lost for Spinoza its nimbus of holiness; he will also know nothing of that Cæsarism, which holds nothing precious in comparison with outward order, or even of that more modern doctrine according to which the man disappears in the member of society, and the latter is raised to the dignity and rank of the substance. If Hobbes gave offence to those of like spirit with himself, by stripping absolutism of the cover of religion, our thinker also finds nothing before which he should bow down in the Republic, the cause of which he pleads. Yet, by the one, human existence is limited to the temporal and external, and eternal salvation itself is nothing more than the reward given hereafter by a despotic God to blind subjection in this life; by the other, the worldly regarded by itself may appear sober and base, but in truth it does not rest upon itself only; it stands everywhere in relation to the eternal, and is subjected to the service of the inner moral life of the individual, aiming—in company with his fellows—at his own perfection.

The man who thus taught appeared to our fathers as the type of a detestable teacher of error. Why is it that we now place him on a pedestal, as one of the wise ones of our race? It is because we have learned to appreciate him, as the type of a free spirit. "Free spirit, free-thinker," these are words of reproach in quarters, where the thought of other men holds the position of truth more than human, to which the mind must bow; but they became titles of honour, where it is recognized that all the thought of which we have cognizance is human thought, and that it is the right and the duty of every reasonable being to obtain convictions of his own. True, Spinoza was still entangled in many a prejudice of scholasticism; whether we ourselves are no longer so entangled, only a later age will be able to decide. Yet in how many respects was he not before his time! How does he reach out his hand to the natural science, to the psychology, to the historical investigation, to the political and moral science of later days! How has he won the gratitude of a Lessing, of a Goethe, as well as of a Schleiermacher; how has he in our days drawn to himself friends, from Russia, Finland, and Sweden, from Scotland, and from Italy, and from the New World! And though we can as little accept his doctrine of the absolute Being as that of Plato or of Aristotle, yet it still maintains its place beside the great creations of his nearest kinsmen in metaphysics, Parmenides and Heraclitus. In quarters where modern science is conjoined with a metaphysical belief, it is his system which furnishes the outlines of the "monism" so much belauded. And yet these are not the principal grounds of our veneration of the man. What chiefly compels our reverence is the attitude he takes up as a free man over against the strict necessary nexus of all things. How many are there whom this thought depresses, and casts down into a cynical view of life, or whom it causes to look back with disquietude to the blessings of the popular faith they have forsaken! But where the old convictions have once died away, they cannot be revived. To renounce the ideals of life would be to prepare for man a lot, compared with which that of the domestic animals might well be envied. The only alternative remaining is to bring the new conviction as to that which is, into harmony with the permanent conviction as to that which ought to be.[44]   In this Spinoza succeeded for himself, and has set up an example for many.   That monster of natural law without pity, from which men recoiled as they had recoiled before from the idea of the earth's motion, and as they still recoil from the idea that life can proceed out of that which is lifeless, this he saw before him undismayed.   He did not regard this law as a strange thing that hemmed him in, or thwarted his aspirations after higher life.   He himself, with all his willing and his doing, had identified himself with this law; he felt himself borne up by all that truly is, and was penetrated by the conviction, that the course of the world-process, being not orderless, but under the rule of eternal law, must be in harmony with the true nature and with the interests of everything that has a place within that process, in spite of all appearances to the contrary.

Thus the builder of one of the most impressive philosophic systems, and the teacher of freedom as we in the Netherlands understand freedom, and as it is coming to be understood more and more all the world over, has in addition to these claims the distinction of being a religious leader, for all those in whose eyes monism and determinism are absolute truth.   For religion is not the daughter of any one view of the world exclusively, or of any one in particular of the classes into which such views may be roughly divided.   It comes to life wherever a pure and fervent heart is filled with the thought of the connection between a man's own being and the deepest basis of all things, in whatever way this basis of all things be represented.   And more than this.   Even where we regard monism and determinism as nothing more than attempts to grasp the absolute under the forms of the relative, the Dutch thinker will still retain in our estimation the garland of a benefactor of humanity, from whom men may learn to preserve, independently of what is changing in their metaphysics, the freshness of their courage, their love to one another, and the eternal life that is in them.

It was mainly for the sake of this lesson that I desired to say in the course of the lectures of this place a word in memory of Spinoza.

NOTES.

1. p. 1. *Baruch de Espinoza* (with short *o*, and *z* = the sharp *th* in English ; a Spanish form (as in Mendoza, Zaragoza) according to the formula of excommunication in Portuguese, published by Van Vloten in the *Supplementum* (see note 8), p. 291. He himself afterwards translated the prænomen, and signed himself "B. de Spinoza." There are, however, Spaniards who write their name *Espinosa*. But it may be mentioned, in favour of the pronunciation just described, that there are Jews at Amsterdam who write the family name occasionally *Spinossa* ⫶ *Cattela*. Boehmer points out that there is a town of the name of Espinosa in Old Castile, and another in the district of Toledo.

In the formula above mentioned Mahamad stands for מעמד, D.B. must be B.D. (בית דין) and K.K. is קהלה קדושה. The date comes to 27th July, 1656.

2. p. 2. Epist. liv. Cogito deinde, me nescire, quibus limitibus libertas ista philosophandi intercludi debeat, ne videar publice stabilitam religionem perturbare velle, etc. His opinion on higher instruction is to be found in the *Tract. Polit.* viii. par. 49.

3. p. 2. The proclamation, which was issued upon the complaint of the curators of the University of Leyden, is printed entire in Van der Linde, *Benedictus Spinoza, Bibliografie.* The Hague, 1871. (No. 24.)

4. p. 3. Pirqé Aboth (in the Mishna), ii. 2.

5. p. 4. Horrendas heregias que practicava *e esinava*, says the formula of excommunication. It was not natural to Spinoza to make a boast of his heterodoxy. He may very conceivably have given private lectures on Descartes, as he did at a later time to a young man who lived in the same house with him at Rhijnsburg (according to some, this was Albert Burgh of Ep. lxxiii. sq.), and interspersed his own remarks, as in the *Cogitata Metaphysica* (Note 6, No. 3) one remark serving to draw out another.

6. p. 5. The titles are :—

(No. 3.) *Renati des Cartes Principiorum Philosophiæ,* pars i. et ii., more geometrico demonstratæ per Benedictum de Spinoza Amstelodamensem. Accesserunt ejusdem *Cogitata Metaphysica,* etc. The writer comes to a stand in the beginning of pars iii., perhaps because the instruction was interrupted at this point. First edition, 1663. Dutch translation, 1664.

(No. 4.) *Tractatus de Intellectus Emendatione,* et do via in qua optime in veram rerum cognitionem dirigitur.

(No. 5.) *Tractatus Theologico-Politicus,* continens dissertationes aliquot, quibus ostenditur libertatem philosophandi non tantum salva pietate et reipublicæ pace posse concedi, sed eandem nisi cum pace reip. ipsaque pietate tolli non posse.

Anonymous, with the false imprint Hamburgi, apud Henricum Künraht (or Künrath). There are four distinct quarto editions, all dated 1670, the two first having *Künraht,* the two others *Künrath.* The three first contain the same table of errata, of which one half is corrected already in the text of II. and III. ; in IV. the text remains as it was, but the table is wanting. For a full account see my paper in the *Transactions of the Royal Academy of Sciences of Amsterdam,* 1881. The false titles of other copies are to be found in Van der Linde (Nos. 4-6) ; see also translation published only after Spinoza's death.

(No. 6.) *Ethica* ordine geometrico demonstrata et in quinque partes distincta, in quibus agitur I. de Deo. II. de natura et origine Mentis. III. de origine et natura Affectuum. IV. de Servitute humana seu de affectuum viribus. V. de potentia intellectus seu de Libertate humana.

(No. 7.) *Tractatus Politicus ;* in quo demonstratur, quomodo societas, ubi imperium monarchicum locum habet, sicut et ea, ubi optimi imperant, debet institui, ne in tyrannidem labatur, et ut pax libertasque civium inviolata mancat.

It appears from No. 5 that Spinoza was in principle a democrat, but without believing in the exclusive saving power of any form of government. The question discussed in that work was the significance of the state in view of the highest interests of the individual; here the subject is the natural history of the state, for which, however, the materials at his command were too scanty. He himself says: Ipsos tamen politicos multo felicius de rebus politicis scripsisse, quam philosophos, dubitari non potest. Nam quoniam experientiam magistram habuerunt, nihil docuerunt quod ab usu remotum esset.

(No. 8.) *Compendium grammatices linguæ Hebrææ.* There is a discussion on this work by Bernays, after Schnarschmidt, Descartes, and Spinoza, Bonn, 1850; and the dissertation of Dr. Ad. Chajes, Breslau, 1869. To Spinoza Hebrew grammar is the foundation of all sound biblical exegesis, which is a thing of the highest consequence for society. (See *Tract. Theol. Polit.* c. 7, and above, p. 37, sq.)

7. p. 6. The theologico-political treatise was proscribed on the complaint of the Dutch synods, in a proclamation dated 19th July, 1674 (not 1671; see Van der Linde, No. 3), and reprinted in Mr. Frederick Pollock's *Spinoza*, p. 444.

8. p. 6. The editions are enumerated in Van der Linde's *Bibliografie*, cited above.

1. *Opera Posthuma* (our Nos. 6, 7, 4, 1, and 8), and the Dutch translation, both at Amsterdam, 1677, and with them a reprint, or edition with new titles, of Nos. 3 and 5, as pars prior.

2. The edition of Paulus, in 2 vols., Jena, 1802-3.

3. That of Gfrörer (without No. 8) in 1 vol., Stuttgart, 1830.

4. The edition of Bruder, in 3 vols. duodecimo, Leipzig, 1843.

5. The supplement of Van Vloten, Amsterdam, 1862, is in the same form, and contained for the first time Nos. 2 and 9, the latter according to the single copy which had been discovered of the old edition, besides a gleaning to be added to the correspondence.—Another MS. of No. 2 was published in 1869 by Prof. Schaarschmidt.

6. The most recent, but also the least satisfactory, reprint is that of Dr. Ginsberg at Leipzig, in four small octavo volumes, at eleven marks.

As the German editions were none of them based on a methodical revision of the text, the Central Committee for the erection of the philosopher's statue resolved to devote the balance remaining on their hands to the printing of a standard edition of his works, the care of which was entrusted to Drs. van Vloten and Land. By collecting and comparing all the available original materials, and with the help and advice of sundry special students of Spinoza, this edition bids fair to satisfy all reasonable expectations, and Mr. Nijhoff of the Hague, as publisher, has taken excellent care of the material execution of the work. The first volume, containing all the principal treatises (Nos. 4, 6, 7, and 5), was issued in May, 1882; the second and last, now in hand, will contain the minor works, the correspondence completed, and with all the names restored, an engraving after the best portrait (now at Wolfenbüttel), and facsimiles in permanent photography of both Latin and Dutch handwriting.

9. p. 6. The later Greek commentators of Aristotle belong to the Neo-Platonic school. It was from them that the Syriac and Arabic students of philosophy received their light, and these in their turn were the guides of the Jewish thinkers of the Middle Ages. The scholastic philosophy of the West was nourished only on Latin commentaries and translations, dating from the latest period of the Western Empire (in addition to Plato's Timæus, and the Christian Neo-Platonist, the pseudo-Dionysius the Areopagite). Afterwards, from the 12th and 13th centuries, Western Scholasticism drew from the complete Aristotle, with Arabic (and among them some Jewish) and Byzantine writers, these also, of course, in translations. Aristotle continued to be the recognized authority for Catholic and Protestant schools down to the 17th century. Even those who refused to follow him had grown up in his ideas, and while feeling it necessary to oppose them, were yet unable in many respects to break loose from them.

Even the terms in which modern discussion is carried on, " form," " matter," " potentiality," " actuality," and others like them, bear witness to the dominant influence of the Aristotelian notions. The old words forma, materia, potentialitas (τὸ δυνάμει εἶναι), actualitas (τὸ ἐνεργείᾳ εἶναι), and so on, are still used, though like the old " idea" (ἰδέα) the dying out of the scholastic tradition has brought to them a change of meaning. Even when the mediæval method still exercised undisputed authority, its terms were beginning to be confused, as for example the confusion of the potentiale with the possibile (τὸ δυνατόν).

4

A lump of copper can become a statue; it is potentialiter a statue : but possibiliter it either becomes a statue or it does not. We may regret the disappearance of the accurate knowledge of an important doctrine, even in quarters where it is regarded as the only true one : yet, on the other hand, what brings about the increasing neglect of the scholastic philosophy is the development of new thoughts. Thus while one scholar makes the progress of science his care, others must labour for an accurate knowledge of her past, and secure by historical inquiry the preservation of what has once been won.

10. p. 8. Descartes does not fully understand the expression, and seeks a meaning for it :—*Meditationes*, ed. Amst. 1698, respons. ad primas objectiones p. 56 sq.: Sed plane admitto aliquid esse posse, in quo sit tanta et tam inexhausta potentia, ut *nullius* unquam *ope egueit* ut existeret, neque etiam nunc ut conservetur ; atque adeo sit *quodammodo* sui causa, Deumque talem esse intelligo . . . Deus . . . videtur *non nimis improprie* dici posse sui causa.

Spinoza also adopts this idea of existence as power. *Eth.* i. prop. 11, schol : Quum posse existere potentia sit, sequitur, quo plus realitatis alicuius rei naturæ competit, eo plus virium a se habere, ut existat, etc. With the Frenchman, however, we find after the definition of the term *causa sui*, the following remark:—Ubi tamen est notandum, non intelligi conservationem quæ fiat per positivum ullum causæ efficientis influxum, sed tantum quod Dei essentia sit talis ut non possit non semper existere. With Spinoza this takes the place of the definition of causa sui : *Eth.* init. : Per c. s. intelligo id, cuius essentia involvit existentiam, sive id, cuius natura non potest concipi nisi existens. This is much more correct, where the metaphysical apparatus is taken from Aristotle. The definition of Descartes reminds us more of Egyptian theology. Compare *Iambl. de Mysteriis*, p. 8, c. 3 : Θεὸς εἷς, πρῶτος καὶ τοῦ πρώτου θεοῦ καὶ βασιλέως, ἀκίνητος ἐν μονότητι τῆς ἑαυτοῦ ἑνότητος μένων . . . παράδειγμα δὲ ἵδρυται τοῦ αὐτοπάτρος αὐτογόνου καὶ μονοπάτορος θεοῦ . . . ἀπὸ δὲ ἑνὸς τούτου ὁ αὐτάρκης θεὸς ἑαυτὸν ἐξέλαμψε, διὸ καὶ αὐτοπάτωρ καὶ αὐτάρκης.

In the *Book of the Dead of Ancient Egypt*, the divine title of Xeper-tésef is explained by " existens per se ipsum." (*Journal of the German Oriental Society*, xxxii. p. 596 note.)

In the notion of God (from the Aristotelian point of view), full existence is involved. From this it follows merely that he who posits such a being must posit it (*inter alia*) as not caused from without and yet as existing. It does not follow that such a being is rightly posited, or that such a being actually exists. This might have been learned from Aristotle himself. *Analyt. Post.*, ii. 7, par. 4; εἰδὼς ἄρα τις ὁρισμῷ τί ἐστιν, εἰ ἐστιν οὐκ εἴσεται, and par. 3 τὸ δ'εἶναι οὐκ οὐσία οὐδενί· οὐ γὰρ γένος τὸ ὄν. In the objections to *Descartes' Meditations*, published after that work, the same argument is used, but in vain. The citations from Aristotle, however, may be met by others in which αἴτιον and αἰτία (causa) serves for the logical ratio or premiss. (*Anal. Post.*, i. 2, par. 5; Soph. *Elench.* 5, par. 9, etc.) Compare also *Sextus Empiricus adv. Mathematicos*, ix. 204; ὅ τε λέγων μὴ εἶναι αἴτιον ἤτοι χωρὶς αἰτίας τοῦτο λέγει ἢ μετά τινος αἰτίας μτλ. Hence in Spinoza *Eth.* i. prop. 33; *Schol.* 1) Rei alicujus existentia vel ex ipsius essentia et definitione, vel ex data causa efficiente necessario sequitur.

11. p. 8. Dr. M. Joel, of Breslau, has furnished important contributions for a knowledge of Spinoza's mediæval Hebrew reading :—

> 1859. *Die Religionsphilosophie des Mose ben Maimon* (Maimonides).
> 1862. *Levi ben Gerson* (Gersonides) *als Religionsphilosoph.*
> 1866. *Don Chasdai Creskas' religionsphilosophische Lehren.*
> 1870. *Spinoza's Theolog.-Politischer Traktat auf seine Quellen geprüft.*
> 1871. *Zur Genesis der Lehre Spinoza's, mit besonderer Berücksichtigung des kurzen Tractats von Gott dem Menschen und dessen Glückseligkeit.*

All these essays are now collected, along with some shorter pieces, in the writer's *Beiträge zur Geschichte der Philosophie*, 2 vols. Breslau, 1876.

The earliest of the series of the thinkers here referred to was the renowned Saadiai, in the first half of the 10th century.

12. p. 10. אור יחוה. I follow the citation of Dr. Joel, in which he has here and there introduced emendations.

עם היות התארים נבדלים בחקנו הם מתאחרים בחקו תארים עצמיים are *attributa essentialia*. Crescas, p. 31, N. 1. Cf. *Eth.* i. def. 4: per attributum intelligo id quod intellectus de substantia percipit tanquam eius essentiam constituens, and def. 6 : per Deum intelligo ens absolute infinitum, hoc est, substantiam

4 *

constantem infinitis attributis, quorum unumquodque æternam et infinitam essentiam exprimit. Prop. 13: Substantia absolute infinita est indivisibilis.

אין שם לא חמר ולא צורח ולא גשמות שלא יהא נאצל ממנו (*Ib.* 66 N. 3). Cf. *Eth.* i. prop. 15: . . nihil sine Deo esse neque concipi potest, and ii. prop. 2: Extensio attributum Dei est.

להיות התחלה שכלית ירצה במה שיצייר "because he is the thinking principle, he wills that which he represents to himself." (*Ib.* 68 N. 3.) Cf. *Eth.* i. prop. 33, schol. 2: . . . nulla profecto sana ratio persuadere nobis potest, ut credamus quod Deus noluerit omnia quæ in suo intellectu sunt, eadem illa perfectione qua ipse intelligit, creare.

אם כן הוא אוהב ההטבה והשפעת הטובה בהכרח "therefore he necessarily loves doing good and communicating (pouring out) good." . . . אין ספק היותו הפועל האמתי לכל הנמצאות בכוונה ורצון "without doubt he is the true bringer about of all that really is, by design and will." *Ib.* 36 N. 1: להיותו טוב תכליתו בעצמו "That he is good has its end in itself." (*Ib.* 63 N. 1.) Cf. *Eth.* i. prop. 16: Ex necessitate divinæ naturæ infinita infinitis modis (h. e. omnia quæ sub intellectum infinitum cadere possunt) sequi debent. Prop. 33: Res nullo alio modo neque alio ordine a Deo produci potuerunt quam productæ sunt. I. Append.: naturam finem nullum sibi præfixum habere. The "good" has with Spinoza no absolute existence; see p. 30.

הנח עם חיותו מורכב מחלקים אשר מזה הוא רבים אין הטוב והשלמות הנמצא לא במה שהוא רבים אלא במה שהוא אחד "Although (the created) is composed of parts, and in so far is a plurality, yet the goodness and the perfection of that which exists lies not in its being a plurality but in its being a unity." (*Ib.* 69 N. 1.) Comp. *Eth.* ii. prop. 40, schol. 2: hoc (tertium) cognoscendi genus procedit ab adæquata idea essentiæ rerum. lib. v. prop. 32: Quidquid intelligimus tertio cognitionis genere, eo delectamur, et quidem concomitante idea Dei tanquam causa.

ולזה לא יצוייר שיהיו שני אנשים על מצב אחד ומזג אחר ותכונה אחת ויחם אחד לדבר בלי חלוף כלל שיבחר האחד מציאותו והאחד העדרו. "Therefore it is not conceivable that there should be two men of one constitution, and one temperament, and one character, and one relation to the same thing, without any difference, and that the one should choose that the thing should be, and the other that it should not be" (*ib.* 48 N. 2). According to the foregoing note the will is determined, and the collective

cause of the will equally so אשר והקבוץ מחייב הרצון היה. Comp. Eth. ii. prop. 48: In הוא סבת הרצון גם כן מחייב
mente nulla est absoluta sive libera voluntas, sed mens ad hoc vel
illud volendum determinatur a causa, quæ etiam ab alia deter-
minata est, et hæc iterum ab alia, et sic in infinitum.

האהבה הוא האחרון התכלית המצווה בבחינת חנה
חטוב הקנאת הוא האחרון התכלית מצוה ובבחינת
השכינה בזיו הנצחי והתרבקות "From the point of view of
him who receives the law, the final end is love, and from the point
of view of the lawgiver the final end is the receiving of good, and
eternal communion with God's glory" (ib. 61 N. 1). Comp.
Eth. v. prop. 36 schol: . . . salus nostra seu beatitudo seu libertas
consistit. . . . in constanti et æterno erga Deum amore.

Spinoza stands on quite a different platform from this believing
member of his race, whom he mentions by name in Ep. xxix.; yet
even these few points on which I have been able to touch testify
to an approach to the doctrine of the unity of essence of God and
the world, the unity of that which is on the one side, and the
pervading causal connection of things on the other side, and also of
the blessedness or perfection that lies in the contemplation of the
one.

13. p. 11. [Baillet], *La Vie de Monsieur Des-Cartes*, Paris,
1691, i. p. 286: . . . S. Thomas qui étoit son auteur favori, et
presque l'unique Théologien qu'il eût jamais voulu étudier.
Descartes, born in 1596, was brought up in the Jesuit college of
La Flèche, a foundation of Henry IV. He then served under
Prince Maurice of Orange and under Tilly, and also later at the
siege of Rochelle, and afterwards lived a life devoted to science in
our country, till he was called by Queen Christina to Stockholm,
where he died in 1650. The first edition of the *Discours sur la
méthode* appeared at Leyden in 1637, that of the *Meditationes* at
Paris in 1641, that of the *Principia* at Amsterdam in 1644, that
of the *Passions de l'âme* at Amsterdam in 1650.

14. p. 13. See the Prize-essay of E. Dühring, *Kritische Geschichte der allgemeinen Principien der Mechanik*, Berl. 1873,
p. 109 sqq.

On Galileo Descartes writes (*Lettres*, Par. 1657-67, T. ii. p. 391):
Je trouue en general qu'il philosophe beaucoup mieux que le
vulgaire, en ce qu'il quitte le plus qu'il peut les erreurs de l'Ecole,
et tâche à examiner les matieres Physiques par des raisons Mathe-

matiques . . . Mais il me semble qu'il manque beaucoup, en ce qu'il ne fait que des digressions, et ne s'arreste point à expliquer suffisamment aucunes matieres ; ce qui monstre qu'il ne les a point toutes examinées par ordre, et que sans avoir consideré les *premieres causes de la Nature,* il a seulement cherché les raisons de quelques effets particuliers, et ainsi qu'il basty sans fondement. P. 394 : Tout ce qu'il dit de la Vitesse des Cors qui descendent dans le vuide, &c. est basty sans fondement ; car il aurait du *auparauant determiner ce que c'est que la pesanteur,* et s'il en sçauoit la verité, il sçauroit qu'elle est *nulle dans le Vuide.* P. 397 : Et premierement touchant Galilée ie vous diray, que ie ne l'ay iamais vû, ny n'ay eu aucune communication auec luy, et que par consequent ie ne sçaurois en auoir emprunté aucune chose, aussi ne vois-ie rien en ses liures, qui me fasse enuie, ny presque rien que ie voulusse auouër pour mien.

Of a " Sr. N.," professor, and our *Simon Stevin,* p. 398 : Il est vray, que ie ne sçay pas ny de l'un ny de l'autre s'ils ont esté exacts en leurs demonstrations ; car ie ne sçaurois avoir la patience de lire tout du long de tels liures. (In the edition of Cousin, the letter here referred to, occurs t. vii. p. 434 suiv. According to MS. notes in a copy preserved in the library of the French institute the date is 8 Oct. 1638.)

15. p. 13. *Christ. Hugenii Opera Varia,* L.B. 1724, p. 721 : Sed tota hæc de cometarum, atque etiam de planetarum et mundi origine, commentatio apud Cartesium tam levibus rationibus contexta est, ut sæpe mirer tantum operæ in talibus concinnandis figmentis eum impendere potuisse.   Huyghens lived from 1629 to 1695. He is the anonymus of Spinoza's *Ep.* xxxix.-xli., whom he consults at the end of the last of these letters on the grinding of glasses.

16. p. 13. *Lettres,* t. i. p. 117 (ed. Cousin t. ix. p. 131) : Et ie puis dire auec verité, que la principale règle que j'ay tou-jours obscruée en mes études, & celle que ie croy m'avoir le plus servy pour acquerir quelque connoissance, a esté, que ie n'ay iamais employé que fort peu d'heures par jour aux pensées qui ocupent l'imagination (*i.e., Mathematics,* see p. 116), & fort peu d'heures par an à celles qui ocupent l'entendement seul (*i.e., Metaphysica, ibid.*), & que i'ay donné tout le reste de mon tems au relasche des sens, & au repos de l'esprit. This last reminds us of Schopenhauer.

17. p. 14. In 1625 he travelled to Loreto (Baillet, i. 120), " pour attirer les grâces de Dieu, et pour se procurer la protection particulière de la Sainte Vierge," according to a vow of Nov. 1619. On this same month we read, i. 63 : C'est à ce tems de repos que nous pourrions assigner l'abdication générale qu'il fit des préjugés de l'école, et les premiers projets qu'il conçût d'une nouvelle philosophie.

In connection with the conversion of Christina (June, 1654), Baillet gives, ii. 433, a testimony of the queen of date 1666, in which she declares that she had in great measure to thank Descartes for it.

18. p. 14. *Lange, Gesch. des Materialismus*, 2te Aufl. i. 202 f., 221 f., raises the question whether Descartes must not have been a materialist at heart, and denied his convictions from fear of the clergy. It is true that he kept back a work entitled *Le Monde* (1633-1634), in order not to be condemned by the Church like Galileo. Yet there is a great difference between silence and accommodation. He was not a priest or teacher whom one expects to declare his views about God, the soul, &c. If he had desired to promulgate heretical opinions on such·subjects, the formulas were ready for his use, as for that of the provost Gassendi and the minim *frater* Mersenne. (Lange, p. 224 sq.) Before his day, Telesio (1508-1588), Pomponazzo (ob. 1525), and others, of an earlier date, had found means of saving themselves by formal subjection to the Church, by drawing distinctions between philosophical and theological truth, &c. Yet why should we not ascribe the inconsistency of such courses to the influence of tradition on the way of thinking of these men themselves? Did the fear of the Inquisition and of public opinion act only on their boldness of speech and not on their boldness of thought as well? The psychology of the coercion of conscience deserves a serious investigation at the hand of the historical student.

19. p. 14. The Italian works of Bruno have been edited anew by Ad. Wagner, Lips. 1829-30. The most important of them is entitled *de la causa, principio et uno*, and first appeared at " Venice " (London? Paris?) in 1584. Αἴτιον, ἀρχή, ἕν are Aristotelian terms, *e.g.*, *Met.* vi. 16 § 4. We read, *i.e.*, p. 261, Wagn.: " Now consider the First and Best Principle, which is all it is capable of being; itself would not be all if it had not the potentiality of being all; in it accordingly actuality and potentiality are the same thing." 264 : " Hence we obtain for the universe a first principle, which is not to be understood as distinctly material or formal any more than may be inferred from its similitude to the aforesaid absolute potentiality and actuality . . . the All is one as to its substance." 269 : " Every essence is by necessity founded upon some being, except the first essence, which is the same with its being " (cp. *Eth.* i. prop. 20 : Dei existentia ejusque essentia unum et idem sunt). 274 : " I say that matter is deprived of forms, and without them, not as ice is without heat, . . . but as the pregnant woman is without her offspring, that she brings forth and quickens by a virtue of her own." 276 : " All things have their origin from matter by way of separation or issue from it, and not by way of adding to it something else which it is to receive ; accordingly, we ought to say rather that it contains the forms and includes them, than that it is void of them and excludes them." 279 : " it (matter) is a divine being in things." 282 : " the universe is all centre, or the centre of the universe is anywhere and the circumference nowhere in so far as it would differ from the centre, or also, the circumference is anywhere, but the centre is not to be found as distinct from it." *Ib.*: " But you may ask : how is it then that things do change, and a particular matter forces itself into other forms ? I answer unto you, that there is not a change into another being, but another *mode* of being. And this is the difference between the universe and the things of the universe, that the one contains full being and all the modes of being, whereas each thing in particular has full being but not all the modes of being." *Ib.* : " In the one infinite, immovable, which is the substance or the *ens*, there is found the plurality, the number, which, as it is a mode and multiformity of the *ens*, distinguishing one thing from another, does not make the *ens* to be more than one, but of many modes, forms, and figures." 283 : " All things are in the universe, and the universe is in all things." 285 : " And that which makes plurality in things, is not the *ens*, nor the cause, but the appearance to the senses, and the outside of the thing." 261 : " The universe (from another point of view) is the great simulacrum, the great image, and the only-begotten nature."

287 : " Would not the most consummate and perfect geometrician be he that succeeded in contracting into one single notion all the notions dispersed in Euclid's principles ; the most perfect logician he that contracted all notions whatever into one. . . . In the same way we that ascend unto perfect knowledge, are continually folding together the plurality of things, as on the other hand, where we take the downward course to the production of things,

the unity is found to unfold itself." 264 : " So you mean to say that, —although in descending by this ladder of nature, there be a twofold substance, one spiritual and one corporeal,—after all both are reduced to one being and one root ? Certainly, if it appear to you that it may be allowed by such as do not penetrate beyond a certain point." 292 : " The highest good, the highest object of desire, the highest perfection, the highest blessedness is in the unity that comprehends the all. . . . As thou, Poliinnio, wouldst delight much more in the unity of a gem so precious as to be worth all the gold of the world, than in the multitude of thousands of thousands of those coins of which thou hast one in thy purse." 275 : " Hence finally, allowing that there be individual things without number, every thing is one, and the knowledge of this unity is the scope and end of all natural philosophies and speculations ; letting alone in its own place that higher speculation which goes beyond nature, the which to any but believers is impossible and non-existing.—So it is, because one attains to it by supernatural, not by natural enlightenment.—Such enlightening they have not who hold every-thing to be a body, either a simple one, as ether, or a compound, as stars and starry things, and seek the deity not outside the infinite world and the infinity of things, but within them."

In another discourse of the same year (*de l'infinito universo e mondi*) Bruno declares, *inter alia* (Wagn. vol. ii., p. 25) : " I say that God is an infinite whole, incapable of any boundaries, and each of his attributes is one and infinite ; and I state God to be totally infinite, because he is wholly in all the world, and in every part of it infinitely and as a whole ; otherwise than the infinity of the universe, which is wholly in the whole, but not in these parts, —provided it be right, with reference to the infinite, to call " parts " such as we are able to distinguish in it." *Ib.* : " On a certain determinate force there follows a certain determinate effect without variation, so that it could not be different from what it is."

It is impossible to think that Spinoza was not acquainted with Bruno. Chr. Sigwart (Spinoza's neuentdeckter Tractat, u. s. w., Gotha, 1866), in a comprehensive discussion of this question (p. 107-134), points out that he made diligent use of Bacon and Hobbes, and yet does not mention their names, except in his letters. And the traces of his agreement with Bruno are still more frequent.

May not Descartes also have been indebted to Bruno for his double substance, his attributes, and modi ?

20. p. 16. In the first Essay (p. 97 sqq. in the Suppl. of V. Vloten), Spinoza distinguishes the notions obtained : 1. Purely from belief ; which belief comes either (*a*) from hearsay, or (*b*) from experience ; 2. from a true belief obtained by true reason, *i.e.*, reasoning ; 3. from a distinct conception. The last is thus described : The fourth, having the clearest knowledge of all, is in no need either of hearsay or of experience or of the art of reasoning, since by its own transparency it at once perceives the proportions in all calculations. The third (No. 2 above) is adequate through the true belief which can never deceive it, and is truly believing ; but the fourth is neither supposing nor believing but beholding the things themselves, not through something else but through the things themselves. So also *De Intell. Emend.* iv. 22 : Per solam denique rei essentiam res percipitur, quando ex eo quod aliquid novi scio, quid hoc sit aliquid nosse, vel ex eo quod novi essentiam animi, scio eam corpori esse unitam. Eadem cognitione novimus duo et tria esse quinque, et si dentur duæ lineæ uni tertiæ parallelæ, eas etiam inter sese parallelas esse. *Eth.* ii. prop. 40, schol. 2 : scientia intuitiva.

The influence of Bruno is here unmistakable. From the Opp. latina of the latter, p. 437, Sigwart quotes (Spinoza's neuentd. Tract. S. 122) the following distinction :—1. *Cognitio sensitiva*, partly outward, partly inward ; 2. *ratio*, nempe potentia qua ex his quæ sensu sunt apprehensa et retenta, aliquid ulterius seu supra sensus infertur sive concluditur etc. ; 3. *intellectus*, qui ea quæ ratio . . . concipit, ipse simplici quodam intuitu recipit et habet . . . et hic est finis ratiocinii sicut possessio est finis acquisitionis et inventionis ; 4. *mens* . . . superior intellectu et omni cognitione, quæ simplici intuitu absque ullo discursu præcedente vel concomitante, vel numero vel distractione omnia comprehendit . . . sicut et mens divina uno actu simplicissimo in se contemplatur omnia simul sine successione ; omnia quippe illi sunt præsentia et nihil cognoscit per peregrinam, sed per propriam speciem omnia . . . omnia in sua substantia. In other passages (*ib.* p. 562 and 595) he distinguishes *sensus, imaginatio, ratio, intellectus*. Intelligibiles species sunt, quibus discursione deposita actu uno possidemus omnia, beati vivimus, æternam mentis intelligentiam imitamur.

Descartes himself had cast a short compendium of his *Meditationes* in the Euclidic form. Spinoza followed him in this in drawing up the little work Note 6, No. 3, and afterwards his own *Ethics*. The first sketch of it, the Essay, has not this form, though it contains two conversations, drawn up at an earlier date, after Bruno.

21. p. 17. *De Intell. Emend.* i. ii., especially ii. 13 sq. : Summum bonum est eo pervenire, ut ille cum aliis individuis, si fieri potest, tali natura fruatur. Quænam autem illa sit natura ostendemus suo loco, nimirum esse cognitionem unionis quam mens cum tota natura habet. Hic est itaque finis ad quem tendo, talem scilicet naturam acquirere, et ut multi mecum eam acquirant conari, hoc est, de mea felicitate etiam est operam dare, ut alii multi idem atque ego intelligant, etc.; utque hoc fiat, necesse est tantum de natura intelligere, quantum sufficit ad talem naturam acquirendam; deinde formare talem societatem, qualis est desideranda ut quam plurimi quam facillime et secure eo perveniant.

22. p. 18. Zwingli, the boldest thinker among the Reformers, goes a long way in this direction. *De Providentia Dei,* cp. 2 (Opp. edd. Schuler et Schulthess, iv. 85 sq.) : Omnis enim virtus aut creata est aut increata. Si increata, deus et numen est; si creata, eam ab illo numine creatam esse oportet. Quæ tamen creata dicitur, quum *omnis virtus numinis virtus* sit: *nec* enim *quicquam est quod non* ex illo, in illo et per illud, *imo illud ipsum sit*—creata, inquam, virtus dicitur, eo quod in novo subjecto et nova specie, universalis aut generalis ista virtus exhibetur. Cp. 3 (p. 87): Quum ergo mundus (ut a philosophis ad me redeam) esse cœperit: fit manifestum almam tellurem non esse ab æterno neque naturâ constare; nisi *naturam* per autonomasiam *numen illud nostrum* intelligas, quod *esse et virtus rerum cunctarum* est, neque in se ipsa esse: ortam igitur atque e nihilo productam oportet. P. 88: Ut ergo rerum omnium prima principia multa credere futile est: sic quicquam esse aut consistere posse, nisi in eo et ex eo sit atque consistat *quod solum est*, rudis est et inexpertæ mentis. Quum enim rebus primo necessarium sit ut sint (nam quid, aut quomodo sint, posteriora sunt); primo quoque datum est eis esse ab illo qui est fons et origo omnium quæ sunt. At esse istud quod rebus ab illo datum est, utrum de suo an de alio mutuo accepit ut daret? Si mutuum est, duo sequuntur incommoda, etc. Si vero *de suo esse* istud accepit quod operibus et creaturis suis dedit, jam *quæcunque sunt ipsum sunt*, in ipso sunt, per ipsum sunt. The prescribed formula " out of nothing " is to be retained : but it is rendered harmless. (P. 87) : Nam hoc est creationis finitio : esse e nihilo ; vel, esse quod prius non fuit, attamen non ex alio tanquam e materia. But according to the above, out of the being of the

Creator himself, which cannot well be made equal to "nothing."
The not being, indeed, was a Platonic and Neo-Platonic expression
for "matter," as compared with "form ;" *e.g.*, Plotin. *Ennead.* ii.
iv. in f : ἡ ὕλη ἡ ἐκεῖ [above] ὄν· τὸ γὰρ πρὸ αὐτῆς ἐπέκεινα ὄντος
[*e.g.*, the form which stands over against it is more than being]
ἐνταῦθα δὲ [here below] τὸ πρὸ αὐτῆς ὄν· οὐκ ὂν ἄρα αὐτή, ἕτερον ὂν
πρὸς τῷ καλῷ τοῦ ὄντος.

The dogma of Calvin is less compliant ; Institut. i. 5 § 6 : Fateor
quidem pie hoc posse dici, modo a pio animo proficiscatur, *Naturam
esse Deum*, sed quia dura est et *impropria loquutio*, quum potius
Natura sit ordo a Deo *præscriptus*, in rebus tanti ponderis, et
quibus debetur singularis religio, involvere confuse Deum cum
inferiore operum suorum cursu, noxium est. How little the
Genevan disciplinarian understood the ruling motive of philosophical thought, is evident from such declarations as this (*ib.*
14 § 1) : At scite pius ille senex quum protervus quispiam ex eo
per ludibrium quæreret, quid ante creatum mundum egisset Deus :
respondit fabricasse inferos curiosis. (A similar anecdote is somewhere told by Luther.) Hæc non minus gravis quam severa
admonitio compescat lasciviam quæ multos titillat, adeoque impellit
ad pravas et noxias speculationes. What would he have said of
such a man as J. S. Mill, who in a similar case said plainly (*Exam.
of Hamilton*, second edition, p. 103) : "I will call no being good
who is not what I mean when I apply that epithet to my fellow-
creatures ; and if such a being can sentence me to hell for not
so calling him, to hell I will go." ?

23. p. 19. *Essay*, p. 81, v. VI. Under " natura naturans," the
Thomists understood God. Sigwart could not find those Thomists,
nor can I. Thomas himself expresses himself differently.
Perhaps Suarez († 1617) is meant. Was Descartes acquainted
with him, or are they the handbook-writers of Coimbra ? The
mode of citation itself shows that Spinoza got the expression from
someone else. From whom ? This question is worth examining, if
we are to get a complete account of his studies.

Encken, *Gesch. der philos. Terminologie*, quotes, as having the
terms, Barthol. Arnold. Using. ep. p. 9, 10, and Meister Eckhart
the mystic. Hauréau, *Hist. de la philos. scolastique*, i. 189, gives
this passage from the Paris MS. of *Heiric of Auxerre* (9th century) :
Deus itaque natura dicitur quod cuncta nasci faciat. Omnis
creatura natura vocatur eo quod nascatur. So the distinction was
clearly conceived long before St. Thomas.

Natura naturata was divided by Spinoza into a general, all the modi which depend immediately on God, and from which alone motion in matter and understanding in thought are known to us, and all the particular things. The division is found in the *Ethics* i. prop. 29 schol. *Natura naturans* there comprises talia substantiæ *attributa* quæ æternam et infinitam essentiam exprimunt; *n. naturata :* omnes Dei attributorum *modos*, quatenus considerantur ut res quæ in Deo sunt et quæ sine Deo nec esse nec concipi possunt. What, however, is meant in prop. 21-23 by the modus qui et necessario et infinitus existit, is not motion or understanding, but the *essentia* of things, distinguished from their *existentia* as individuals.

"Thought and extension" are terms of the translated Essay. How the *Ethics* grew out of this work may be read in Sigwart. My aim was to give a hasty sketch of the doctrine as completed.

24. p. 19. *Essay*, p. 27, v. VI. : . . . " to a being which has some reality attributes must be ascribed : and the more reality is imputed to it, the more attributes must be ascribed to it ; and consequently if the being is infinite, its attributes must also be infinite ; and it is just this that we call an infinite being." *Eth.* i. prop. 9 : Quo plus realitatis aut esse unaquæque res habet, eo plura attributa ipsi competunt.

25. p. 19. *Joël* (Spinoza, S. 42) translates from Abraham Shalom († 1492) as follows :—" Chasdai simply combines two contradictory opposites, when he says that the *necessary* genesis of the world from God comes about in the way of will, since God is an intelligent cause, and therefore wills that which he conceives " (נוח שלום cap. 15). Compare supra, note 12.

26. p. 20. *De Intell. Emend.* iii.: 1. Ad captum vulgi loqui, et illa omnia operari, quæ nihil impedimenti adferunt, quo minus nostrum scopum attingamus.

" Ratio seu causa," " causa seu ratio," " ratio nec causa datur," especially in *Eth.* i. prop. 11, demonstr. 2.

27. p. 20. Otherwise he might have been content (if at least he meant to make the one side of existence depend on the other) with the scholastic expression, " ratio sufficiens *essendi* " (*Eth.* i. prop. 24 coroll.), in opposition to " ratio sufficiens *fiendi* " (the ordinary " cause," or " causa efficiens "), and " ratio sufficiens *cognoscendi*."

(*Arist. Metaph.* Δ. 1) : ἀρχή = τὸ πρῶτον ὅθεν ἢ ἐστιν ἢ γίγνεται ἢ γιγνώσκεται.

We see the confusion which still adhered to him in *Eth.* i. prop. 33, schol. 1 : Rei enim alicuius *existentia vel* ex ipsius *essentia et definitione, vel* ex data *causa efficiente* necessario sequitur.

Spinoza's view was shared in this instance by Leibnitz (*Nouv. Ess.* b. iv. ch. 17) : la raison est la vérité connue, dont la liaison avec une autre moins connue fait donner notre assentiment à la dernière. Mais particulièrement et par excellence on l'appelle raison si c'est la cause non seulement de notre jugement, mais encore de la vérité même, ce qu'on appelle aussi raison *à priori* et la cause dans les choses répond à la raison dans les vérités.

For his meaning as to God as cause, see prop. 17, schol.: Verum ego me satis clare ostendisse puto, a summa Dei potentia sive infinita natura infinita infinitis modus, hoc est, omnia necessario effluxisse, vel semper eadem necessitate sequi ; *eodem modo*, ac ex natura trianguli ab æterno et in æternum sequitur, eius tres angulos æquari duobus rectis.

28. p. 21. It is too frequently forgotten that geometry does not proceed, like arithmetic, (algebra comes here under the head of arithmetic) by pure logical deduction, but by the contemplation of figures constructed in the imagination. The first elements for these constructions we derive from the perception which makes us acquainted with objects in space. Thus we are tied in the construction, among other things, to a space of three dimensions (length, breadth, depth). Space manifests itself everywhere and always in the same way, and every perception in which three dimensions are involved yields all the elements necessary. Hence the appearance with regard to geometry, that it is built up by purely logical deduction. Analytical geometry, of which Descartes is the discoverer, treats relations between geometrical magnitudes by purely algebraical methods; and this also gives occasion for a misunderstanding of the nature of geometry. Yet the treatment applies to the relations only in so far as they are relations between magnitudes; the geometrical character of these is pre-supposed, but is not expressed in the formulas, which could be applied equally well to magnitudes of another kind. See my article, "Kant's Space and Modern Mathematics," in *Mind*, January, 1877.

Spinoza can maintain that the relation between God and the world is of the same nature as that between mathematical data, and may yet proceed illegitimately in concluding that the world must "follow" from God, or in asserting that the notion of God can be developed to knowledge of the world by purely logical process—since here we cannot have that imagination which, with the abstract definition of the notion to guide it, should construct an object which the mind can look at and examine from different sides as if it were a mathematical figure.

29. p. 23. *Cog. Metaph.* ii. c. 1, par. 4: Atque hanc infinitam existentiam æternitatem voco, quæ soli Deo tribuenda non vero ulli rei creatæ; non, inquam, quamvis earum duratio utroque careat fine. *Eth.* i. prop. 33, schol. 2: . . . quum in æterno non detur *quando*, nec *ante*, nec *post.* v. prop. 23 : . . . menti humanæ nullam durationem quæ tempore definiri potest tribuimus . . . . nisi durante corpore. Quum tamen aliquid nihilo minus sit, quod æterna quadam necessitate per ipsam Dei essentiam concipitur, erit necessario hoc aliquid, quod ad mentis essentiam pertinet æternum.

30. p. 24. Jacobi, *Works*, iv. a. p. 44 (*Elise Reimarus*) . . . . " the system of Spinoza generally accounted an atheistic system." *Ib.* p. 216 (Jacobi). " Spinozism is Atheism."

Walch in his *Philos. Lexicon*, Leipz. 1740, calls Spinoza an atheist, and also mentions him as a representative of modern materialism.

Hegel, *Encyclop.* par. 50 (*Works*, vi. p. 110): " it is involved in this unity . . . . that in the Spinozistic system the world is rather made a mere phenomenon, to which no true reality can be ascribed, so that the system is rather to be regarded as *Acosmism.*" Comp. *Vorles. über die Gesch. der Philosophie*, iii. p. 361. The same remark had been made in 1802 by C. Th. de Murr, in his edition of the philosopher's notes to the *Tract. Theol.-politicus*, and even before him by Moses Mendelssohn. In the preface to the posthumous works of Christoph Wittichius (= het Onderzoek van de zede-Konst van B. de Spinoza) in Sepp, *Godgel. Onderwijs*, ii. 373: mundi θέωσις est Spinozismi prora ac puppis; Renatæ (Renati Castesii) Philosophiæ est, Deum distinguere a mundo.

The late Karl Thomas (for a list of his earlier writings on Spinoza, see v. d. Linde) assures us in a posthumous work that here we have two things—two masses of thought, which cannot be thoroughly compared with each other, are with studied art interwoven by Spinoza in his *Ethics :* first, the mystic monistic Pantheism of Spinozism, and secondly the atomistic-automatic

Pantheism of Spinoza (*Herbart—Spinoza—Kant*, Langensalza, 1875, p. xiii.).

Were it worth while, this list might be lengthened out with hundreds of quotations. The worst sneerers at Spinoza (excepting the fanatical sort of theologians) have been the school of Herbart, from their master (in the *Allgem. Metaphysik*) to O. Flügel (*die Problemeder Philosophie und ihre Lösungen*, Cöthen, 1876). They require the absolute Being in the plural, and resent Spinoza's assertion: determinatio est negatio (*Ep.* v.) with which he cuts off, they say, a multiplicity of substances, since the one would not be what the others are. This argument had been used before by the Eleatics (Aristot. *Metaph.* ii. 4, par. 26 τὸ γὰρ ἔτερον τοῦ ὄντος οὐκ ἔστιν κτλ). The assertion is certainly used in support of Spinoza's one infinite substance (*Eth.* i. prop. 8, cum scholiis), but the true origin of the latter is to be found in Jewish speculations on the dogma of creation. It was evidently this dogma along with the Aristotelian doctrine of matter and form which led Bruno to think. Spinoza borrowed from him and from Descartes other forms than those suggested to him by his Hebrew reading. But making the claim he did to an adequate knowledge of God's essence, (*Eth.* iv. 47) he could not declare with Bruno that the absolute is only comprehended as a denial of all relativity.

(*De la causa*, etc. I. p. 263 Wagn.): "This most absolute actuality, which is the same with the most absolute potentiality, cannot be comprehended by the intellect otherwise than by the way of negation; I mean to say that it cannot be understood either in so far as it is capable of being all, or in so far as it is all."

31. p. 25. Our fellow-countryman J. B. Lehmann (*Spinoza, sein Lebensbild, etc.* Würzburg, 1864) thinks it incomprehensible (p. 112) how the term law of nature was introduced into Spinoza's doctrine, since a law without a lawgiver is a contradictio in adjecto, and Spinoza with plain words rejected a lawgiver, *i.e.* a Creator who calls things into existence with reason and will. But even νόμος and lex have the signification, "custom, accepted rule:" the notion of regular recurrence, not that of being ordained by some one, is here the chief point. Even in antiquity the term was transferred from social order to the order, for example, in nature.

32. p. 25. The notion of self-sameness (identity) gives occasion for misunderstanding as well as that of cause. Two things or more must always be supposed, before they can be declared identical. The meaning of this is, that an object is in one respect a unity, while in another respect it is seen to be more than one, or may be so regarded ; it being understood that unity belongs to the object as a thing thought by itself, plurality to the object in its manifestation to the beholder. $3 + 5 = 8$ signifies : that which appears as a sum of 3 and 5, and also, in another connection of ideas, as the well known term in the series of numbers which we call 8, is in reality, *i.e.* apart from the manner in which we apprehend it, only one magnitude, and not two. Thus we read, *Eth.* ii. prop. 7, schol.: substantia cogitans et substantia extensa una eademque est substantia, quæ jam sub hoc jam sub illo attributo *comprehenditur.* Sic etiam modus extensionis et idea illius modi una eademque est *res :* sed duobus modis *expressa.* Hence the discussion of the expounders of our thinker on the question, whether the plurality of attributes is in his view real, or simply in appearance, for our understanding. Compare Busolt, *die Grundzüge der Erkenntnisstheorie und Metaphysik Spinoza's.* Berlin, 1875, p. 107 sqq. In the case of the identity of God and the world, on the other hand, we have to think of another relation in connection with the doctrine. It is not like the relation between $3 + 5$ and 8, but as that between the actual magnitude and its quality as $3 + 5$ or as 8. The magnitude is one definite magnitude ; but also it is $3 + 5$, it is 8, it is $7 + 1$, it is ⅛, etc. And thus the substance is one and undivided, and yet, on the other hand, res cogitans, res extensa (II. prop. 1, 2) ; it is also constans infinitis attributis (I. prop. 11) ; and equally, that in which are all the modi (I. prop. 15). Here we have also to consider that to Spinoza the modi themselves are more than appearances to us, and exist independently of our apprehension. The sharp distinction between the object before the mind, and the absolutely real, which to us is almost self-evident, is not made at the standpoint of the older metaphysics, which thus become entangled in difficulties not to be removed by even the most careful study of the sources. To speak plainly : that which is combines in itself, according to Spinoza, qualities which to the reason are conflicting, unity and plurality, eternity and changeableness ; in one respect it is God, in the other it is the world. And more than this : the members of which as a plurality it consists from the first, such as thought and extension, or Being in thought and Being in space, must not be understood as parts (see *Eth.* 1, prop. 12), but as one being that is at the same time thought and extension. What there is in this that we cannot accept is due to the effort to apply the notion of substance to the absolute, and may be laid to the charge (*mutatis mutandis*) of all dogmatic philosophy.

In the essay on God, etc. these attributes still bring about the one in the other, as with Descartes, by mediation of the spirits (*spiritus animales*, as people still speak of, "someone having plenty of animal spirits"): the soul has "operations in or upon the body" (pp. 187-189, v. Vloten) : yet along with this we already find the doctrine (pp. 185-187) that "no manner of thought can bring any motion or rest into the body;" and that "the soul, being an image of the body, is itself so united with it, that in this way they make a whole together."

33. p. 26. *Eth.* ii. prop. 23 : Mens se ipsam non cognoscit, nisi quatenus corporis affectionum ideas percipit.

34. p. 26. Bain, *The Senses and the Intellect*, 2nd ed. p. 625 : I was anxious to do away with the supposed distinction between states of feeling accompanied with bodily manifestations, and states not accompanied with such manifestations, which distinction I believe to be erroneous. Wundt, *Physiologische Psychologie*, ii. 862. . . . that the soul is the inner being of the same unity which outwardly we behold as the body belonging to it. . . . To every outward change there corresponds a change of the inner state.

35. p. 27. Descartes had already made the remark : Simulac quis aliquid scit, eo ipso scit se id scire, et simul scit quod sciat, et sic in infinitum. Spin. *Eth.* ii. prop. 43 : Qui veram habet ideam, simul scit se veram habere ideam, nec de rei veritate potest dubitare, etc.

36. p. 27. A professor at Leyden, b. 1625, died, too soon, 1669. I have not yet been able to obtain the original of his *Metaphysica vera et ad mentem peripateticam* (Amst. 1691, 12mo.). The old folio catalogue of our library does not even contain his name ; a few of his works were afterwards procured for it. I thus quote the unique copy of the Dutch translation (Dordregt, 1696) in my own possession. *Metaph. Gerund. Perip.* p. 1, note : "We are not right in considering things as they appear to the senses or to the intellect, and we are not able to consider them as they are in themselves; from which our imperfection becomes manifest. Hence this one thing remains for us to observe, as often as we come to comprehend anything under any one of our modes of understanding (which, as long as we are men, we are always compelled to do): namely, in every instance to be mindful that the thing in itself is not such as it is taken by us to be. Although we always apply the appearances and intellectual species to the things themselves, nevertheless there is something divine in us which tells us that it is not so, and in this all our wisdom will consist as long as we are human beings." P. 2 text: "Objects of the senses are distinguished by philosophy from the forms and appearances which the senses are wont to confer upon them, and so they are considered by true philosophy in Physics. But such things as are not objects of sense, she distinguishes and separates from the modes of our understanding, and from the *phasmata* and *species intellectuales;* for our mind, as few seem to be aware, is no less prone to put its ways of thinking upon the objects of its thought, than the senses to impute their own imaginations to the things that they lay hold of; and those things divested of the intellectual species are considered by true philosophy in Metaphysics." P. 3: "As children see a stick half immerged in water as if it were broken, not only with their eyes, for so even men cannot help seeing it, but with their mind, by which they show that they are children indeed, led astray by the prejudices of their senses, and often make us smile; even so the Peripatetics are like children, attributing with as little right their modes of understanding to the things understood; not only with their mind, for so do the true philosophers as well; but even with the judgment of their rational understanding; calling, yea believing and maintaining, things in themselves to be substances, or accidents, or qualities, or relations, or wholes, or parts, etc. . . . . all of which cannot apply to the things, but is entirely dependent on the modes of our intelligence. It is merely, as one might say, "our own talk, by which nothing is decided or influenced in reality." Attention was drawn to this doctrine a few years ago in Germany by Ed. Grimm, *Geulinx', Erkenntnisstheorie und Occasionalismus*, Jena, 1875.

37. p. 28. Even Bruno mentions somewhere " the desire of self-conservation which impels everything as an internal principle." " Il desio di conservarsi, il quale spinge ogni cosa come principio intrinseco." Telesio (de Rerum Natura IX. c. 3) says : Hominum spiritus, qualiscumque sit, entium animaliumque reliquorum ritu se ipsum conservandi propriamque operationem operandi, motus nimirum edendi seseque iis oblectandi, se ipsum omnino conservandi omnino est appetens. C. 4 : . . . eo usque scilicet afficiendus commovendusque est spiritus, et eousque iuxta affectus operandum

spiritui est, dum quæ editur operatio eius conservationem procuret
et spiritum omnino conservet : malum vero ubi illa inferre incipit,
vel operationes quibus conservatur perficiturve spiritus, impedit,
vel iucundissima quæ sit, et ad spiritus conservationem perfec-
tionemve necessaria, edendo, et tamdiu omnino, quamdiu spiritus
conservationi perfectionive bona est commodaque : non a voluptate
omnino ad operandum impellendus, neque a dolore ab operationibus
reiiciendus, sed a sui ipsius conservatione utrumque.   C. 29 : . . .
eaque entia bona visa sunt quæ a tanta ac tali natura constituta
sunt, a quali quantaque eius generis entia constituenda sunt, a
propria nimirum puraque et sincera, nihilque alienis commixta ab
alienisque passa, . . . utique entium virtutem eorum puritatem
esse liquido patet.

Bruno's Italian writings appeared in 1584: the complete work of
Telesio in 1586. We read in the former of "il giudizosissimo Telesio
Consentino" (*De la Causa*, p. 250 w) ; this must refer to the two
first books, printed in 1565. Spinoza probably knew something
of Telesio ; the doctrine regarding agere and pati, in particular, in
the third part of the Ethics, may have been drawn from that
source. If so, the "suum esse conservare" and "in suo esse
perseverare" may also have been borrowed from him.

38. p. 31. Jacobi in his conversation with Lessing (Jacobi's
W. W. iv. a. 71). " Spinoza also had to stoop not a little to conceal
his fatalism in its application to human conduct, in his fourth and
fifth parts, where I should be inclined to say that he here and
there lowers himself to the level of a sophist." Jacobi declares
indeed, p. 223 : " Every way of demonstration issues in fatalism."

39. p. 33. Spinoza was no foe to the Christianity to which his
friends the Collegiants and Baptists looked for their salvation ; he
was of service to his landlord at Voorburg in connection with an
election in the Reformed Church there ; and he conversed with the
inmates of the house, where he died, on the subject of their worship,
for which he testified great respect. The system of compulsory
belief, however, of the Romish and non-Romish authorities with
their following, he summarily rejected. His writings show that
he had read the New Testament with edification. Yet he draws
an essential distinction between those who seek their salvation
through philosophy and those who seek it through Biblical religion.
His express separation from Christian doctrine is plain from
his distinct denial of a personal God, of sin, and of redemption

through a saviour. The psychological basis of his doctrine of love is that which is its foundation all the world over—his own love to man : this he has in common with Jews and Christians, as well as Buddhists who do not know the traditions of Bible doctrine. The theoretical basis on which he seeks to rest it, and which leads to its modifications in detail, was naturally a different one from that of the various religious teachers of Asia and Europe, who built on other premisses.

40. p. 35. In the Neo-Platonic commentators on Aristotle, the existing definitions of philosophy are enumerated ; among these (*e.g. David Armenius,* p. 13 to 45 *Scholl. Berolin*), μελέτη θανάτου. Plato had said (*Phædo,* 67 D), τὸ μελέτημα τοῦτ' ἐστὶ τῶν φιλοσόφων, λύσις καὶ χωρισμὸς ψυχῆς ἀπὸ σώματος. Hence with the later Stoics (*Porphyr. Prolegg. Philos. Scholl. Ber.,* p. 76, 28), μελέτη τοῦ φυσικοῦ θανάτου. Spinoza, not being aware of the historical origin of the definition, appears to think, *Eth.* iv. prop. 67, of man's dread of the Last Judgment.

41. p. 36. In the one, where he makes the νοῦς or λόγος in us have part in the eternity of the ideas, though its immortality is further defined as pre-existence and imperishableness. In the other, in the doctrine of the νοῦς ποιητικός, the divine element in the human soul, not capable of any change of state, which, it is true, is introduced into it from without, yet reminds us in so far of the mind of Spinoza, which is the divine and incorruptible in man, while the νοῦς παθητικός, standing related to it as matter to form, along with all the lower elements, passes away at the same time with the body.

42. p. 37. The theological learning which Spinoza requires in the teacher of the people, has thus, to use the term stamped by the theologians, a "rationalistic" character. His view is more or less akin to that of Thomasius, of Wolf, and of Kant. Kant, for example, finds the essence of religion in the "fulfilment of all human duties as divine commands." Spinoza, however, does not, like Kant, force exegesis under the yoke of morals. ("This inter-pretation may often seem forced when confronted with the text—the revelation—and may often be so : and yet if the text will admit of it, it must be preferred to a literal interpretation which either yields nothing at all for morality, or even matter against it." (*Werke* x. 131, *Rosenkr.*) In place of the pastoral twisting of the

text in the interests of edification he makes choice of a purely
historical investigation, convinced that by this method there will
be sifted out from the temporary and personal elements peculiar to
each individual writer, the permanent and universal elements in
which succeeding generations also can find refreshment.

43. p. 39. The political doctrine of Hobbes (1588-1679) is set
forth in his books *De Cive* (1642) and *Leviathan* (1651). The
following citations are taken from the Amsterdam edition of 1668
(two volumes, small quarto, Jo. Blaeu) :—

De Cive, p. 8 : Lex naturæ signifies " dictamen rectæ rationis
circa ea quæ agenda vel omittenda sunt ad vitæ membrorumque
conservationem quantum fieri potest diuturnam." P. 6 : Æquales
sunt qui æqualia contra se invicem possunt. Sunt igitur homines
natura inter se æquales. In statu naturæ silent leges naturæ.
P. 52 : No difference between tyrannis and monarchia legitima.
P. 55 : monarchia a potestate populi derivatur, scil. jus summum,
hoc est, summum imperium, in unum hominem transferentis.
P. 52 : siquidem in civitate democratica vel aristocratica summum
imperium civis aliquis vi occuparet, civium consensu, legitimus fit
monarcha (*coup d'état* with confirmatory *suffrage universel*) ; eo
consensu non habito, hostis est, non tyrannus.

To the supreme power is ascribed whatever contributes to the
preservation of order : justice, the right to make war, legislation
(the décrets of the great Napoleon), the nomination of all officials,
inviolability, independence of the law (the divorce of Jerome
Bonaparte by an arbitrary sentence of his brother) and power to
suppress mischievous opinions (censorship of the press under the
Empire). Then also the power to teach. *Leviath.* p. 120 : populum
enim docendi monarchis solis et cœtibus summis auctoritas a Deo
immediate concessa est, ut qui soli dicantur simpliciter Dei gratia
docere et imperare (Napoleon's *Université de France*). *De Cive*,
p. 43 : sequitur ergo illum unum . . . hoc quoque habere juris, ut et
judicet quæ opiniones et doctrinæ paci inimicæ sunt (*sic*), et vetet
ne doceantur. *Lev.* p. 1 : Magnus ille Leviathan, quæ Civitas
appellatur, opificium artis est, et homo artificialis . . . . In quo
qui summam habet potestatem pro *anima* est, corpus totum vivifi-
cante et movente . . . . Divitiæ singularium hominum sunt pro
robore.   P. 85 : the Leviathan is also called Mortalis Deus;
cui pacem et protectionem ut deo immortali debemus omnem.
The comparison with the Bonapartist state might be carried
further.

Against this Spinoza *Epist.* L: Quantum ad politicam spectat, discrimen inter me et Hobbesium, de quo interrogas, in hoc consistit, quod ego naturale ius semper sartum tectumque conservo, quodque supremo magistratui in qualibet urbe non plus in subditos iuris, quam iuxta mensuram potestatis, qua subditum superat, competere statuo, quod in statu naturali semper locum habet. The newer doctrine spoken of is not the renewal of the antique which was based on the deification of the state, and thus on the mythical way of thinking. Aristotle also says on occasion (*Polit.* I. 1): ἡ πόλις καὶ φύσει καὶ πρότερον ἢ ἕκαστος. Yet he also says (III. 1): ᾧ ἐξουσία κοινωνεῖν ἀρχῆς βουλευτικῆς ἢ κριτικῆς, πολίτην λέγομεν εἶναι . . ., πόλιν δὲ τὸ τῶν τοιούτων πλῆθος ἱκανὸν πρὸς αὐτάρκειαν ζωῆς. It is natural to man to live in the state: this is all he means.

Hobbes on religion, *e.g.*, *Lev.* p. 28: Metus potentiarum invisibilium, sive fictæ illæ sint, sive ab historiis acceptæ sint publice, religio est; si publice acceptæ non sint, superstitio. Quando autem potentiæ illæ revera tales sunt quales accepimus, Vera Religio. *De Cive*, p. 166 sq.: Prodest ad scientiam explicatio nominum, quibus id quod inquirendum est, proponitur, imo unica via ad scientiam est per definitiones; ad fidem autem nocet hoc. Nam quæ supra captum hominum credenda proponuntur, nunquam explicatione evidentiora, sed contra obscuriora et creditu difficiliora fiunt. Acciditque homini qui mysteria fidei ratione naturali conatur demonstrare, idem quod ægroto, qui pilulas salubres sed amaras vult prius mandere quam in stomachum demittere; ex quo fit ut statim revomantur, quæ alioquin devoratæ eum sanassent.

Against this Spinoza, *e.g. Tract. Theol.-pol. c.* 15: Verum quidem est Scripturam per Scripturam explicandam esse, quandiu de solo orationum sensu et mente prophetarum laboramus: sed postquam verum sensum eruimus, necessario judicio et ratione utendum, ut ipsi assensum præbeamus, etc. C. 20: nihil reip. tutius, quam ut pietas et religio in solo caritatis et æquitatis exercitio comprehendatur, et jus summarum potestatum tam circa sacra, quam profana ad actiones tantum referatur; ceterum unicuique et sentire quæ velit, et quæ sentiat dicere concedatur.

44. p. 44. There is a difference, too much overlooked, between our way of thinking as to the constitution of things, and that as to the relation borne by the constitution of things to the claims our mind naturally makes on things. The second admits of great variety, irrespectively of the first, according as our consciousness of these claims has been developed in one way or another. The doctrine, for example, of a personal being by whose will the world was made and whose providence watches over all, is commonly felt to be full of comfort, indeed indispensable: and accordingly we see it passionately defended. Yet it happens sometimes that this doctrine is held simply because one has been brought up in it, and has found no reason as yet for doubting it, who yet cannot reconcile himself to a deity who must have willed the pain and evil that are in the world. The doctrine of duty as a divine command, which might have been other than it is, confers to many minds a higher sanction on the sense of duty; others stumble at the arbitrary prescription of duties which, as daily experience teaches us, cannot be adequately discharged by such beings as we are. The Christian doctrine of satisfaction provides relief for many who are oppressed by the burden of their sins: others cannot reconcile themselves to the suffering of an innocent person, and the readiness of the eternal guardian of the moral law to accept the vindication of its dignity from any quarter, while the law itself remains unfulfilled.

Thus it comes to pass, that great points of the doctrine of the Church, even when a man can bring forward no objection to the truth of them, yet produce any effect on him rather than that of a saving revelation. From this position to that of unbelief in dogma there is but a single step, though a step which is not taken in every case. Those who find their satisfaction in dogma are indignant at this state of things: they think the present generation ought to feel the same wants as the generation in the past by whom the dogma was brought out. A little inquiry, however, would show that even materialism, pantheism, atheism, and other such ways of thinking, in which the majority can see nothing but backsliding and perversity, have mostly an ethical impulse, and draw strength from the fact that a man will accept from an impersonal nature-power, what cannot content him if coming from the hands of a personal being, of infinite wisdom and love. Or the advantage of the newer system in the eyes of some may consist in the difference they see between the service of an ideal law, not to be shaken because it is rooted in human nature itself, and that of a lawgiver and governor of the world, with whom there may be negotiation.

Whether a theoretical conviction makes men blessed or miserable depends not so much on its contents as on the spirit in which it is entertained. If it is forced upon us by authority or by tradition, or if our examination of existing things leads us to regard it as an object external to ourselves, then it will easily come in conflict with our personal aspirations which have grown up apart from it. If, on the other hand, the one and the other have grown up in us together, if we have always regarded the subject, our own ego, as an element in the great whole which we conceive, then we feel ourselves at home in that whole, and the life of our mind is a life of harmony. Such a harmony may be cultivated by art, carrying on a special training to cause the claims of the mind to accommodate themselves from the earliest years to some particular dogma. How poorly this system answers in the long run we see, *e.g.*, in the results of orthodox instruction in France, Spain, Italy, Russia, precisely in the most cultivated classes. It is a more excellent way when the thinking part of a society has its attention steadily directed to the intimate connection which subsists between our true interests and the constitution of the whole of which nature has made us a part. This can be done in very various ways, according to the idea that is given of the whole. In any case, however, a change in the explanation of the nature of the connection will not endanger the thought, which alone is essential for our peace of mind, of its existence. What issues from this thought, and gives us moral support, is the religious life (not from *religare*, but from *religere*, " to respect," take account of; comp. *intelligere*, "inspect;" *religentem esse oportet*, the old poet says, *religiosum nefas*, *i.e.*, man must not be superstitious but must bear constantly in mind his relation to a higher being.

The Buddhist also is religious, though not God-serving. He regards himself as one with the genus of the self-determining person who, as Buddha is held to have proved by his example, can withdraw himself from the torment of continuance in the world of changing things. By such a view earthly life receives for him a consecration, which would not satisfy us, but nevertheless renders happy him who has once raised himself to the required standpoint, and which strengthens him in many universally recognized virtues. Compare Koeppen, *Die Religion des Buddha*, Berl. 1857, p. 296 sq.: "What thou art and wilt be, what thou hast and findest, joy and sorrow, beauty and ugliness, power and lowliness, poverty and riches, birth and death, all are simply the fruits of thy own doing. Thou reapest only what thou thyself hast sowed. To the sin-darkened, unenlightened eye, it is true, the law of retribution according to a man's own works (here filling the place of a general law of nature) seems to be a strange power, external to himself, of which he can give no account." . . . . The Buddhist self-determination, however, is capable of being turned against itself, by the resolve henceforward no more to will or to act, and thus to break the chain of the consequences of works. By this means the individual is freed from the burden of existence. The Buddha stands directly opposite to Spinoza : his eternal becoming, it is true, without any true being is directly opposed to Spinoza's eternal substance. Yet he also finds an opening for the individual to obtain salvation and blessedness, by identifying himself with that which remains with him as the eternal basis of all beings : the power to determine one's own lot. Contrary to what some would expect, the doctrine of independent personality here issues in self-annihilation, or at least retirement from the world; while the doctrine of necessity of our European thinker leads to cheerful taking up of what our hand finds to do in this world! So we may learn from his example to judge of the moral effect of a theory, not from the light in which it presents itself to outsiders accustomed to different views of life, but in connection with the entire development of thought to which it essentially belongs.

II.

THE LIFE AND CHARACTER

OF

BARUCH SPINOZA:

A LECTURE

BY

KUNO FISCHER,

PROFESSOR OF PHILOSOPHY AT BERLIN.

TRANSLATED BY

FRIDA SCHMIDT.

THE LIFE AND CHARACTER OF
BARUCH SPINOZA.

---

*　　*　　*　　*　　*　　*

WHAT I wish to describe is the secluded and solitary
life of a lonely man—a life devoted to no other aim save
that of pure thought—as far as it can be revealed, and is
capable of disclosing itself to outward view. But how
little does the outward view reach the essence of such
a life! How apparently poor and monotonous are the
external aspects of a life entirely devoted to contemplation!
The stirring events, the numerous exciting, varied, and
striking incidents, which attract the imagination and sup-
ply the most grateful theme to the narrator, are wanting.
To appreciate the quiet life of a thinker, we must regard
it from within. And that which never ceases to interest
and instruct the student of human nature, who thus looks
at it, is the harmony of the tendency of thought with the
tendency of action, the reciprocal and mutually regulating
effect of thought and life upon each other. Such a harmo-
nious combination produces one of those rare characters
which are at rest in themselves, which are made of one
stuff throughout, and which live and act exactly as they
think.

I am well aware in what an unfavourable position I am placed, when I now attempt to set before you the life and character of one of the choicest of these men, without being able at present to throw light upon that inner world of thought in which he lived.

I.

SPINOZA'S HISTORICAL SIGNIFICANCE.

I shall try therefore, whether, in a few words, I can indicate that tendency of thought, which was one with the tendency of personal life, in the character I endeavour to describe.

It was part of the task of that new era, which was endeavouring to free itself from the trammels of the Middle Ages, to lay anew the foundations, not only of religion, but also of knowledge and science, each upon its own peculiar basis—religion upon the Scriptures, science upon natural Reason. One of the greatest thinkers of the world, the man who first undertook this reform in the sphere of philosophy, René Descartes, had boldly said : "The thing must all be done over again from the beginning. Nothing that has not been perceived as clear and self-evident must be accounted as true ; only what is clearly and self-evidently perceived is true." Now the clearest and most self-evident kind of knowledge which we have is the science of mathematics in its unquestionable certainty, its rigid and inevitable sequence. As clear, as certain, as logical must all our knowledge be. If it is less so, then that degree of clearness and self-evidence which completely excludes doubt, and which alone has a right to the name of truth, is wanting. Whatever you do not think and comprehend as clearly as the proposition that the sum of the angles of any triangle is equal to two right angles, you do not comprehend at all!

It is therefore an essential feature of the spirit and aim of the new philosophy which has come down to us from Descartes, that it sets before itself the problem of regulating the entire realm of knowledge according to mathematical necessity, and of bringing everything in the world into a chain of mathematical sequence, in which each link follows the other as plainly as the links in a mathematical proposition. Philosophy, it is said, must be proved *more geometrico*. Here we are at the point, so weighty and momentous in the history of philosophy, at which it is confronted by this problem, and where the solution of this problem is its next task—a task which may not be avoided, and where the attempt at solution must be made thoroughly and in its whole extent, even though such an attempt may only tend to show how many things there are in the world which do not admit of being mathematically proved. Such negative results are as important as the positive ones, and often far more fruitful.

We can understand this problem, independently of the systems of philosophy, through the direct experience of our own mind. Who has not, at some time of his life when the mind began to assert itself in bold self-confidence, been conscious of the demand: "I must prove everything as clearly as the proposition two and two make four; whatever is less clear to me than this must be reckoned as unproved, and, so far as science goes, must count for nothing!" This demand will often be heard again. In philosophy it has met with its fulfilment, it has had its day. Only once in the world has it been met actually, seriously, and completely so far as this was possible; and that was by *Baruch Spinoza.*

In order to make this demand, scarcely anything more is needed than the self-assurance of the aspiring mind, growing in self-confidence in itself, and for the first time feeling its own power. But in order systematically and seriously to carry it out an unconquerable strength of mind and will is required, which has equanimity enough to hold out against the contradiction of the whole world. In this respect Spinoza's philosophy and character are an unexampled and unique phenomenon. Not merely magnitudes but things, not merely the physical world but the intellectual life of humanity, he explained according to mathematical method. He has a geometrical theology, a geometrical moral philosophy; and he disowns everything that will not conform to this standard.*

There is one notion which refuses to enter into mathematical thought, which does not fit into this mode of thinking. It would be absurd to ask, for what purpose are the angles of the triangle equal to two right angles? for what purpose are the radii of a circle equal? for what purpose does twice two make four? In these cases the only question to be asked is, why are these things so? Mathematical truths have only causes; they have no purposes.

If then, all truths followed the law of mathematical necessity, there could be no purpose at all. Purpose would be an absurdity, an indistinct and confused idea, a mere unsubstantial imagination. There would be neither natural, nor moral, nor Divine purposes. The foundation upon which ancient philosophy, Christian

* See my *History of Modern Philosophy,* vol. iii., book i., chap. i., p. 7.

theology, and the generally prevailing view of the world rest, must be declared invalid. If we add to this that the first philosophers of the new period who preceded Spinoza—such as Bacon and Descartes—did not altogether deny validity to the notion of purpose, decidedly as they excluded it from the physical explanation of things; and that philosophers subsequent to him—such as Leibnitz and Kant—again asserted the validity of this conception, then Spinoza's position in the world is indeed unique, completely isolated, opposed to the leading thinkers of earlier as well as of later times.

He stands solitary; solitary in his thoughts, and solitary and forsaken in his life. In fact a perfect witness to the truth as it shone in upon his own mind, and as, according to the exigencies of that period of philosophical development, it had to be thought. Shall I call it a thing of chance that, then, when philosophy needed and called for a system which should place her in the most pronounced opposition to the received ideas of the world, it was to an excommunicated Jew that she confided herself, and her cause?

II.

The Underlying Moral Tendency.

" I look at human actions entirely as if I were dealing with lines, surfaces, and bodies." This utterance characterizes the man and his mode of thought. "I have accustomed myself to look upon human passions, such as love, hatred, anger, envy, ambition, compassion, and all the other emotions of the soul, not as faults of human nature, but as qualities which belong to it, just in the same way as heat, cold, storm, thunder, and other similar phenomena belong to the nature of the atmosphere, which may indeed be inconvenient, but which are necessary, and which have certain causes."

In this way of thinking things are estimated only as they are in themselves. It is considered that they cannot be otherwise, cannot be either better or worse. They have no purposes, therefore they ·can fail in none. Defeated purposes are pitiable, or ridiculous—according as we take them. In Spinoza's view there is nothing that could or should be different from what it actually is, nothing accordingly at which one should seriously weep or laugh. Hence that famous saying, which many have repeated after him, but which no one carried out as he did, "we must neither mourn over things, nor laugh at them, but understand them."

People call things bad or good, in the same way as they call the weather or the season bad or good, that is, according as these are favourable or unfavourable to themselves. They judge things as the peasant in the fable judged the acorn: "what a pity for the acorn that it is not a gourd." And when the acorn falls down then they say: "Thank heavens that it was not a gourd." Here we see the stupid habit which everywhere prevails, and leads men to estimate things according to their own wishes and desires. This way of thinking is in fact selfish, and hence in what it calls its judgments, in which it takes credit for being wonderfully critical, it arrives at no more profound conclusion than that the acorn is not a gourd. So does folly judge all things, that is to say, so does the multitude judge!

The whole work of Spinoza's life was directed to one point: he sought to free himself from self-deception, and its delusions. This work was withal his deepest personal necessity. He perceived that the root of self-deception is selfishness, which creates the tribe of our appetites, wishes, and passions. As long as our mind is imprisoned and blinded by them, it is quite incapable of recognizing the truth. If we call love the opposite of selfishness, then the love of truth was the one ruling and enlightening motive in his life and character. His whole existence was a self-renunciation for the sake of this love.

At the very beginning of his first work, we see the whole man, and the direction to which his life and philosophy tended. Descartes begins with the confession: "I have held much to be true, which I now discover to be false, I have no reason to suppose anything to be more certain. Possibly everything that I conceive and believe is false. What then is true? What is certain?" Spinoza begins with the confession: "I have held much to be good, which I now discover to be vain and worthless. I have no reason to suppose any one of the so-called goods of life to be any better. Possibly they are all merely apparent goods—possibly everything that men are accustomed to wish for and long after is vain and worthless. What then is good? What is the true good, the good which is real and imperishable? Any good that I possess engenders in me a pleasurable feeling, is the cause of contentment and joy to me. If then there is any good, which is perfectly real and incapable of being lost—if it is possible to strive for and win such a good—then the contentment that it would bring me would be lasting and indestructible, my joy would be eternal." This good cannot be obtained in the same way in which we seek and attain the ordinary transitory goods of life. It is not possible to strive for these and for that good at the same time. The paths that lead to them are different. One or other must be abandoned, either the eternal good or the temporal, either the good or the goods. Whichever of these paths a man chooses, he must renounce one of them, and he must make up his mind to decide upon this renunciation, when he has clearly seen its full significance. In Spinoza's mind the question was not merely the solution of a problem, it was the choice of a *life's aim.*

This resolution must be taken in perfect calm and clearness. It is not an easy one to take; the weighing of the eternal good against the temporal is not so simple and certain as it may seem. If we were sure of the eternal, if it lay before us so that we could grasp it in our hands, then the choice would not be difficult! Who would not prefer the lasting to the transitory joy? But in the first place, that eternal good is a mere supposition, and a very problematical one! The question is: does such a good exist? can it be won and possessed by us? Whether this good really exists, and exists for us, is uncertain. It lies in the meantime in obscurity. On the other hand, the goods of life lie before us in distinct and enticing proximity. Though they are transitory yet they are certain, or at least they appear far more certain than that eternal good, of which we do not know what and where it is. Shall we, then, quit the path towards the certain attainable enticing goal, to take the other towards an uncertain and perhaps impossible goal? Shall we give up the certain goods for the sake of the uncertain?

What are they, these so-called certain goods? They may be all reduced to these three: enjoyment of the senses—wealth—distinction. In truth, these goods of life which are desired as the most certain, change, when one thoroughly examines them, into pure losses. They are nothing but apparent goods, phantoms which carry decay within themselves. What we really get from them are delusions and stupefaction, disgust, loss of liberty, want, and disappointment.

Thus, on considering the matter aright, we have to choose between an uncertain good and a host of certain and undoubted evils. Can the choice be any longer doubtful? The choice which has on the one side certain death and on the other the possibility of cure. There, the prospect of decay; here, the prospect of life! This is plainly our only hope, our only possible deliverance. " For I saw," said Spinoza, "that I was in the greatest danger and that I must seek with all my strength for a means of recovery, even though it were but a doubtful one. Just as a man sick to death, when nothing else avails, seizes with all his energy even upon a remedy which is uncertain, for in it lies his whole hope. All those goods put together which the multitude runs to pursue, not only can do nothing for the preservation of our existence, but they actually hinder it. They are frequently to blame for the ruin of those who possess them; they are always to blame for the ruin of those who are possessed by them."

This is the consideration which brings to a head Spinoza's resolution to let go the goods of life and to strive for the incorruptible good. So his first work begins with the confession: " Experience having taught me that everything that usually goes to fill up men's life is vain and worthless, and as I saw that all the causes and objects of my fear were neither good nor bad in themselves, and only became so according to the effect they produce on the mind, I resolved at last to try whether there were not one true and attainable good with which the mind could occupy itself to the exclusion of everything else ; and whether indeed anything could be found the possession of which would for ever ensure the most lasting and the highest joy."

Whence then come those desires which vex us, and put us out of tune, such as grief, fear, hatred, envy, etc. ? They all spring from the same source—our love of what is transitory. With the vanishing of this love the whole tribe of our desires vanishes. " If these things were no more loved, strife would no longer arise, there would be no mourning when they were destroyed, no envy when another possessed them, no fear, no hatred; in one word, there would be none of those emotions which all alike proceed from the love we bear to temporal things." That good, then, the love of which ought to fill the soul to the exclusion of all else, can be nothing but an eternal and unending being. " The love of an eternal and unending being," says Spinoza, " fills the soul with a joy that shuts out every kind of sadness. Such a state is to be desired most earnestly and to be sought for with the whole soul."* It is the love of truth which thus lays hold of the heart of man and purifies it from its desires.

III.

THE MORAL TYPE.

Thus Spinoza became a moral type—unrecognized indeed by his contemporaries, because they shrank from the teaching of the man as from the head of a Medusa ; yet, the ideal he presented touched and penetrated a

* The first work of Spinoza, the *Tractatus de intellectus emendatione*, from the beginning of which these quotations are taken, has unfortunately remained fragmentary.

number of the noblest spirits of succeeding generations, especially in Germany.

Lessing, who was always at hand when there was a character to be rehabilitated, drew attention to Spinoza, as he had already done to Shakespeare. "Even up to this day they speak of him as of a dead dog," he said in that famous and important controversy with Jacobi. He felt himself so akin to Spinoza in his love of truth, that he declared that his cause was his own, and that he was intellectually a brother of Spinoza, so that the idea arose that Lessing was a Spinozist.

In a certain sense Goethe really was one. To get rid of his passions in a loving contemplation of nature, and in undisturbed sympathy with her, was to this poet a necessity and a blessing. Such a devotion to the truth of things, such a frame of mind, so free from desire and so transparent, he felt to be a lifting of life to a higher level, a renewal and consecration of energy. He says himself, that he has cooled his burning brow in the peaceful air, which Spinoza's spirit always breathed on him. It is to Truth that the confession in his *Zueignung* is addressed :—

> "Yes, I have felt thy influence oft, I cried,
>   And sank to earth before her, half adoring,
> Thou brought'st me rest, when Passion's lava tide,
>   Through my young veins like liquid fire was pouring.
> And thou hast fanned, as with celestial pinions,
>   In summer's heat, my parch'd and fever'd brow,
> Gav'st me the choicest gifts of earth's dominions,
>   And save through thee, I seek no fortune now."

This passionless mood, when the pressure of desire is relaxed, and the mind turns of its own motion to the pure contemplation of things and to the cognition of the

eternal, has been expressed by Goethe in his *Faust* in the
true spirit of Spinoza :—

> " Now lulled to sleep is wild Desire,
>   And stormy deeds that Passion brings,
>   The Love of God with holy fire
>   Springs up, the Love of man upsprings."

The mood which underlies Spinoza's philosophy is a
religious one.   For his doctrine shares with religion
these two essential tendencies :—deliverance from selfishness, devotion to the eternal !

This explains why Schleiermacher, when dealing in his
lectures on religion with the great theme, that not in
ideas nor in propositions, but in the soul alone does
religion dwell,—felt himself so overpowered in connection with this subject by the memory of Spinoza, that he
exclaimed :—" When philosophers become religious and
seek God as Spinoza did, and when artists become pious
and seek Christ as Novalis did, then will be celebrated
the great resurrection for both worlds.   Humbly offer
a lock of hair to the manes of that holy excommunicated Spinoza.   He was penetrated by the great
Spirit of the universe, the Infinite was his beginning
and end, the Universe his one and everlasting love.
Therefore he stands alone and unequalled—master in his
art, but exalted above the ordinary guilds — without
disciples, without citizenship."

And Friedrich Heinrich Jacobi, who revived the
knowledge of Spinoza, although he was his greatest
opponent in philosophy—and that on religious grounds—
yet recognizes that the germ of life at the centre of
Spinoza's doctrine is a religious one.   " Blessed be thou,
thou great, yea, thou holy Benedictus !   However, thou
mayest have philosophized on the nature of the Highest

Being, and lost thyself in words, yet his truth was in thy soul, and his love was in thy life."

I shall now give an outline of Spinoza's simple and touching history.

IV.

Biographical Sources.

(Bayle, Kortholt, Colerus, Lucas, Boullainvilliers.)

Spinoza lived in so complete a seclusion from the world, that those outside could have but little knowledge of the man. It was not to be looked for that any one should know him so well as to be able to give a true and complete picture of him to posterity. To this we may add that the details of the eventful experience of his youth are enveloped in an obscurity, which none of his biographers have been able to clear away. Hence only the outlines of the events of Spinoza's life could be narrated; and even these from records, drawn from meagre and diverse sources, and which when pieced together, left many gaps unfilled. The trustworthiness of these accounts is questionable in more than one particular. Religious party zeal has mixed itself up with some parts of the narrative of the philosopher's history; and the polemic and apologetic interests, which Spinoza's teaching excited, have contributed—each from its own side—to distort and mystify even the simplest facts of his life.

The first insignificant sketch of his life was given by Peter Bayle in his *Encyclopedia*. So far as this article goes, that work does not deserve the title which it bears of *Critical-Historical*. This sketch was translated into Dutch by F. Halma in 1698.

Two years later there appeared a pamphlet by Christian Kortholt, Professor of the Reformed theology, entitled, *The three great impostors.** It was well known that in the Middle Ages, a book bearing the same title, and considered as the very extreme of heresy had been written against the founders of the three Monotheistic religions —Moses, Christ, Mohammed. Kortholt directed his book against the three naturalistic philosophers, Herbert, Hobbes, Spinoza. One sentence will be sufficient to exhibit the spirit of this book, and to show at the same time how witty Kortholt could be on occasion. He is furious because Spinoza had taken the name of Benedictus, the Latin translation of the Hebrew Baruch: " He should rather have been called Maledictus (the accursed one), for according to the divine curse in the first book of Moses, the thorny earth (Spinoza terra) has never borne a more cursed man than this Spinoza, whose works are bestrewed with so many thorns (*spinis*). The man was first a Jew, but being excommunicated by the Synagogue (ἀποσυνάγωγος), he finally, through I know not what intrigues and wiles made his way among the Christians, and called himself by their name." The truth is, that although Spinoza left Judaism, he never either openly or in secret went over to Christianity.

Sebastian Kortholt, the son of the above writer, added to this book a preface containing several statements regarding the life of Spinoza, which the author says he had collected at the Hague from the lips of trustworthy and well-informed persons. He calls Spinoza bluntly the Atheist. Kortholt relates, that he sometimes gave private lessons, without taking any payment for them,

* *De tribus impostoribus magnis.* Hamburgi, 1700.

and to this he adds a reason; "for mischief could be had from him for nothing."

The most important, and in his way the best, biographer of Spinoza is Johannes Colerus, minister of the Lutheran Church at the Hague. He set himself with care to the task, and reported faithfully all that he was able to hear of the philosopher's life down to the smallest and most insignificant incidents. His narrative is chiefly drawn from oral sources. It was easy for him to collect information in this direct way, because he lived at the Hague in the house of the widow Van Velden, where Spinoza had lodged formerly; and, moreover, had personal intercourse with the artist, Van der Spyck, under whose roof the philosopher had spent the last part of his life. Colerus is often shocked with Spinoza's doctrines, but he is at the same time so evidently impressed by the philosopher's moral purity, his modest unselfishness, the simple grandeur of his character, that one might think that his picture had been drawn by a friendly hand. He first published the life of Spinoza in Dutch, along with a sermon refuting Spinoza's allegorical explanation of the resurrection of Jesus. In the same year the biography appeared in French.* The zeal of Colerus against the philosopher whose doctrine he rejects, never carries him into malice against his person; yet in spite of all the human sympathy he feels for him, he cannot approve of his being called "blessed" after his death. The occasion on which Colerus protests against this expression is almost ludicrous. He says, "I will remark by the way

---

* *La vie de B. Spinoza*, tirée des écrits de ce fameux philosophe et de temoignage de plusieurs personnes dignes de foi, qui l'ont connu particulièrement, par Jean Colerus, ministre de l'église lu thérienne de la Hague, 1700.

that after Spinoza's death his barber brought an account which ran : 'Herr Spinoza of blessed memory owes the surgeon Abraham Kernel for his services during the last three months, one florin eighteen sous.' The sexton and two tailors paid the deceased a similar compliment in their bills. If these good people had known what religious principles this Spinoza had, they would very likely not have used the phrase so lightly. Or did they only use it because custom sometimes permits the misuse of such words even for those persons who have died in despair and impenitence ?" And yet this same Colerus states shortly before this, that all the reports of the despairing death of Spinoza were nothing but lies, and that his end was as quiet and gentle as his life.

This biography appeared afterwards in German. The translator gave vent to his fanaticism in a peculiar fashion. Since he could cast no stain upon the fair character drawn by Colerus, he prefixed to the book a picture of Spinoza distorted into a caricature, with the inscription underneath, *characterem in vultu gerens.* " He bears the brand of reprobation on his brow."*

A second apologetic writing is entitled, *Life and Spirit of Spinoza.* The biographical part treats Spinoza as a kind of saint. The didatic part is a worthless compilation. The author was said to be the notorious Doctor Lucas, at the Hague. Only a few copies of this work were printed, and it very soon became rare and dear. It was subsequently circulated in manuscript, and the first part of it was republished under the title : *The life of Spinoza by one of his pupils.*†

---

* *Das Leben des B. von Spinoza aus den Schriften dieses berufenem Weltweisen,* u. s. f. 1733.

† *La vie et l'esprit de Mr. Benoît de Spinosa,* 1719. La vie de

These two biographical sources were uncritically mixed up together in a third work published by Fénélon, Lami, and Boullainvilliers.*

V.

THE PORTUGUESE JEWS IN AMSTERDAM.

The victorious struggle of the Netherlands against the Spanish rule created in the liberated country a platform of civil and religious liberty which afforded a secure, auspicious, and much-needed shelter for the unimpeded development of faith and knowledge. Descartes served his first campaign in Holland, which was then allied to France, and afterwards found there that quiet leisure whence issued the works containing his new system. The oppressed and the persecuted of other lands—especially those who suffered on account of their faith—assembled from all quarters in this home of liberty. The same tendency, so early as the beginning of the 17th century, brought into the Netherlands crowds of Jews, who were threatened by the Inquisition in Spain. The "Portuguese Jews," as they were called, founded in this shelter a new community, whose centre was the synagogue of Amsterdam. A remark which Spinoza

Spinosa par un de ses disciples; nouvelle édition non tronquée, augmentée de quelque notes et du catalogue de ses écrits par un autre de ses disciples. Hambourg, 1735.

* *Réfutation des erreurs de Benoît de Spinosa*, par Mr. de Fénélon, archevêque de Cambray, par le P. Lami Benedictin, et par le comte Boullainvilliers, avec la vie de Spinosa écrite par M. J. Colerus, augmentée de beaucoup de particularités, tirées d'une vie manuscrite faite par un de ses amis. Bruxelles, 1731.

[To these may be added the two works recently published by Van Vloten: *Baruch d'Espinoza, ziju Leven en Schriften.* Amst. 1862. *Ad B. de Spinoza opera quæ supersunt omnia, supplementum.* Amst. 1862. Ed.]

himself casually makes in his theologico-political treatise explains why these Jews were called specially the Portuguese Jews. " The Jews of the Pyrenean peninsula," so runs his remark, " were forced either to become Catholic or to emigrate. In Spain these converts obtained full civil rights and mixed with the Spanish nation. In Portugal, on the contrary, they were isolated and excluded from all participation in public affairs ; consequently they there preserved unchanged the peculiarities of their national character."* In a short time this school of Amsterdam rose into such estimation that it might be considered a principal seat of European Judaism. It seemed as if the great period of the Jewish Middle Ages, which had developed itself during the 12th and 13th centuries in Spain, was now to bring forth a second bloom in the Netherlands. About the middle of the 17th century the newly founded community had risen to its full power and importance.

The refuge of the persecuted easily comes to be viewed as a refuge for free movement of mind in every direction. Under the protection of Dutch liberty the synagogue of Amsterdam—itself a leading school of Jewish and oriental wisdom and erudition—became independent, and secure against all assaults from the ecclesiastical and political powers of Christendom. It also possessed an attraction for those who had fallen out of relations with Christianity, and who were threatened with clerical persecution. Spanish Christians left their own country to go over to Judaism at Amsterdam. One of them, Uriel Acosta, became by his fate a tragic personage. Through the struggles he underwent with the synagogue, and the persecution which arose against him from the side of

* *Tractatus theologico-politicus.* Cap. iii.

fanatical Jewish orthodoxy, he was so far the predecessor of Spinoza. When the hatred of his fellow
believers drove him to despair, and he put an end to his
life, Spinoza was a boy of fifteen years, and the first
among the younger Jewish Talmudists of Amsterdam.

VI.

Spinoza's Family. His Hebrew Education.

1. *His Parents.*

In the midst of this Portuguese community Baruch
Spinoza (d'Espinosa) was born on the 24th of November,
1632, at Amsterdam, in a house on the Burgwall, near
the old Portuguese synagogue. He had two sisters,
Rebecca and Miriam. The elder of the two remained
unmarried, the second married a man of her own faith,
Samuel Carceris. Spinoza's parents were respectable
merchants; they gave a careful education to their only
son, whose extraordinary abilities they soon observed,
and destined him for the vocation of a Jewish scholar.
According to Lucas, his parents were not rich enough to
make their son a merchant. According to Sebastian
Kortholt, their son determined, in defiance of his father's
will, that he would be a Rabbi. Neither account seems
very probable. Whatever may have been the pecuniary
circumstances of the parents, these would not have
debarred their son from a mercantile career; and would
not a pious and faithful Jew—such as Spinoza's father
doubtless was—have rejoiced to see in his son a future
light of the synagogue, especially as he had reason to be
convinced of that son's mental endowments?

2. *The Rabbinical School.*

However this may have been, it is certain that Baruch

Spinoza entered on the career of a scholar, and went through
all the stages of the Rabbinical School, from the elements
of Hebrew up to the Scriptures of the Old Testament,
particularly the Pentateuch and the Prophets; from these
he passed on to the Talmud, and thus to an acquaintance
with the Jewish commentators and schoolmen of the
Middle Ages, among whom Maimonides was the chief.
This wide domain of Jewish theology Spinoza, eager for
knowledge, explored thoroughly, and with untiring zeal.
His teacher, Saul Levi Morteira, was one of the greatest
Talmudists of his time; his name was the first among
the Rabbis in Amsterdam, and he himself was the founder
of a theological school. In a short time Spinoza was
known as so conspicuous and learned a scholar, that he
became the pride of his teacher, and the hope of the
synagogue.

3. *The Cabbala.*

In addition to the Old Testament and the Talmud,
he studied the Cabbalistic books out of which a later
Jewish wisdom developed a theosophic system—related
to the Mosaic faith in the same way as Gnosticism is to
Christianity, and as Neoplatonism is to the Greek pagan
religion. It is well known of what importance the
Cabbalistic lore has been, since the days of Pico of
Mirandola and Reuchlin, in the transition from scholasticism to the revival of philosophy. Between the theological spirit of the Middle Ages, and the rationalistic spirit
of the new philosophy, theosophy forms a necessary and
important transitional stage. It was at this point that
the Cabbala entered in a striking and effective way
into the scientific development of Christian thought.
Spinoza was thus unconsciously led by the hand of Jewish
literature to the threshold of the new philosophy. I do

not mean by this to say that the Cabbala was a kind of preparatory school for Philosophy to him, still less, that his own doctrines were derived from those of the Cabbala. Some such connection has been talked of at times, and some have sought to include the philosopher Spinoza among the Cabbalists; thus bringing him back through the secret door of the Cabbala to that Judaism, which expelled him from the synagogue. Why is not Descartes made a Cabbalist as well! All this talk only proves that those who indulge in it understand nothing of the real character of Cabbalistic wisdom, and still less of Spinoza's doctrine and style of mind. Neither do they know how Spinoza himself regarded the Cabbalists. Here is his own declaration regarding them: "I have likewise read several Cabbalistic babblers, and have never ceased to marvel at their nonsense."*

He studied the whole field of Jewish theology and theosophy, and the final result was that he tore himself away from them, profoundly dissatisfied. Instead of a Rabbi, he had become a Sceptic. He thirsted for the knowledge of God and of Nature, and this thirst was not quenched by Old Testament, Talmud, or Cabbala.

VII.

THE RUPTURE WITH JUDAISM.

1. *The Estrangement.*

For the first philosophers of the new period it is a hard struggle to attain to that independence which is necessary for looking at things as they are, apart from all preconceived notions. Their youth and education are

---

* Tract. *Theologico-politicus*, cap. ix. (Ed. Paulus I, p. 297).

given over to the power of tradition, which, with its sacred authority and its massive scholastic wisdom, takes prisoner their judgment and early subdues the freedom of their spirit. Descartes, in the Jesuit's school of La Flèche; Spinoza, in the Rabbinical school of Amsterdam! The first a pupil of the strictest and severest order as regards Papal authority, the other a disciple of the Talmud! But so it has to be! The only real independence is that gained in a struggle with difficulties. Both men learned thoroughly what they could learn; both obtained the mastery over the subjects which they studied; both were admired as scholars, and at the end of their course their minds were entirely estranged from the spirit of the school which had trained them—a spirit which they saw to be far beneath them.

We have no confessions of Spinoza, either by word of mouth or in writing, to give us an insight into the inward struggles through which he must have passed in the Rabbinical school, while he gradually came to the decision which destroyed all possibility of mental sympathy between him and the synagogue. I do not think that these struggles were of a stormy nature. His clear, intelligent brain sought light, and found darkness. He desired truth and knowledge, and the riper he grew the plainer must it have become to him, that the whole Jewish wisdom had quite another basis than that of science; that the Cabbalistic books were far removed from a clear conception of things, and that the Mosaic law was not in any way qualified to afford scientific views of things. He attained this conviction with great clearness and it quietly strengthened within him. He perceived in the Scriptures of the Old Testament a string of contradictions, a want of connection and agreement, which must have necessarily shaken his belief in the homage which the Jewish faith paid to these its documents. Such scruples must have been awakened while he still had before him the prospect of the Rabbinical vocation. For after having explained his scruples in his theologico-political treatise, he explicitly says : "I write nothing here that I did not think over long ago, and that I have not thought for a long time."* His need for knowledge makes him struggle out of the realm of the Rabbis to find at last the longed for light in the works of Descartes. The Talmudist becomes a philosopher, and the Sceptic a Cartesian, the keenest and most powerful of them all.

2. *The Conflicts.*

Spinoza's transition from Jewish theology to Descartes and to philosophy—a transition which developed and completed itself in the stillness of his own soul—was accompanied by a terrible catastrophe, which shattered his outward life. Disputes arose between him and his instructors, and these at last led to a breach with the synagogue, which solemnly excommunicated him as an apostate.

We know little about the particular circumstances which preceded and accompanied this final measure. So much is certain, that the synagogue did everything in their power to prevent an open rupture. On the other hand, we may be sure that little as Spinoza may have feared such a catastrophe, he would not in any way challenge it. It was not his nature to provoke violent scenes ; but still less would his character, which had its centre in the love of truth, ever allow him to seem different from what he really was. No kind of hypocrisy

* Tract. *Theologico-Politicus*, cap. ix.

was possible to him. · After his mind had renounced sympathy with the synagogue, he felt that he could no longer remain outwardly connected with it. His visits to the synagogue became rarer, and he ceased to take part in its worship. This silent separation was at first the only tangible sign that he gave of his change of mind. But he was of too much consequence in the eyes of the synagogue, the object of hopes too important, for his withdrawal to pass unnoticed. The Jews were afraid of losing this distinguished thinker, perhaps even to the hostile religion.

Great men always call forth, in the circle which surrounds them, the jealousy of those whom they involuntarily cast into the shade, and who do not like to be thus obscured. We may be certain that among Spinoza's co-religionists—especially among the learned who stood nearest to him—envious feelings would be roused, and envious eyes would watch him. Among the passions which kindle and inflame the spirit of persecution, the base emotions are never wanting ; and of these, envy is the basest, the most unjust, and at the same time the most active.

The idea at first seems to have been to draw out Spinoza, and thus discover his real state of mind. Two pretended friends undertook, either on their own responsibility or in obedience to a hint from some higher quarter, to involve him in a snare. They led him into a discussion about the nature of God, the immortality of the soul, the reality of angels. They wished him to tell them whether God had a corporeal nature—whether the soul was immortal, and whether the angels were real beings. Spinoza tried to avoid their conversation by answering : "Ye have Moses and the prophets." But as they pressed him further, and seemed to be actuated by a real desire for knowledge, he frankly explained his position; and showed that, according to the Bible, God could be regarded as corporeal, the angels as apparitions, the soul as a mere principle of life. They tried repeatedly to draw him out, but he remained silent.

Then evil reports began to be circulated about his belief. He was called a godless blasphemer, a despiser of the Mosaic law—of which he was said to have affirmed that its basis was to be found in political purposes, and not in a knowledge of God and of nature. He was summoned before the bar of the Jewish tribunal to answer for his belief, tried, exhorted to repentance, and threatened with excommunication. Neither efforts to convert him, nor threats, nor bribery could move him. He was already the object of such bitter and excited passions that attempts were being made on his life. Bayle relates that when he was leaving the theatre, a Jew attacked him, and wounded him in the face with a knife. Spinoza himself tells this story differently, and it was his version that Colerus heard from the painter, Van der Spyck. One evening as he was coming out of the old Portuguese synagogue, he noticed quite close to him a man with a dagger in his hand. He was on his guard at once, and avoided the thrust, which pierced through his clothes. In remembrance of this event Spinoza kept the garment which had been cut. This fact, so confirmed, cannot be questioned. But one feels rather inclined to ask how it happened that in the midst of these conflicts Spinoza should still have attended the synagogue? After such an attack he could no longer feel himself safe in Amsterdam, and it is probable that it was at this time that he sought a refuge outside the city.

The Rabbi Morteira himself is said to have hastened
to the synagogue, and after vain attempts to convert
Spinoza or to persuade him to recant, overwhelmed his
favourite pupil with curses. The particular details of
this scene which Boullainvilliers relates are evidently
false and invented. We are entitled to presume that
in his judicial examination Spinoza would declare his
opinions with the greatest decision and fearlessness, and
that there would be none of that school-boyishness and
insolent defiance which the narrative of Boullainvilliers
ascribes to him. All attempts at conversion, and all
threats addressed to him were unavailing.

Another expedient was tried, in order that at least he
might retain the name, if not the creed of Judaism. The
Rabbis offered him a pension of a thousand florins if he
would remain a Jew and occasionally attend the synagogue. This fact is undoubted. Spinoza himself often
told it to the artist Van der Spyck, from whom Colerus
heard it. He added that he never would have accepted
this offer, even if it had been ten times as great, for he
was, he said, no hypocrite, and he sought not money but
truth.

3. *The Anathema.*

As the attempts to gain him or destroy him had all
failed, the last resource that remained was to shut him out
from the congregation—the formal anathema. The Jewish
form of anathema has three degrees—Niddui, Cherem,
Schammatha. The first degree inflicts banishment for a
certain time, in the first instance for thirty days. In the
second the banishment is accompanied with a maledic-
tion; and in the third every evil is invoked on the
blasphemer's head. The older Talmudists distinguish
only two degrees, and regard Cherem as the highest,

while they consider that Schammatha is merely a different name for the first degree. The greatest crime of which Spinoza was declared guilty was blasphemy—contempt of the law. Hence Colerus thinks that it was Schammatha, or the great ban, which the old Rabbi Chacham Abuabh* publicly pronounced upon Spinoza. Colerus was not able to find out any particulars regarding this affair. Neither did he succeed in procuring from the sons of the Rabbi the record containing the terms of the curse pronounced against Spinoza. They pretended that they were unable to find it among their father's papers, but it was evident that they did not wish to produce it. The document has been brought to light quite recently through the exertions of Van Vloten. It was on the 6th of August, 1656, that the following anathema against Spinoza was read in the synagogue of Amsterdam :—

" The lords of the spiritual council do you to wit that they, having been long aware of the godless sentiments and words of Baruch Spinoza, have endeavoured on various occasions and with promises to turn him from his evil ways. But since they could do nothing with him, but, on the contrary, had daily greater experience of the frightful errors which he manifested by word and deed, and of his shameless utterances—in proof of which they had a number of trustworthy witnesses, who in his presence gave their testimony, and brought these things home to him—therefore they have resolved, in presence of the Rabbis and with their concurrence, to pass this sentence of excommunication on this Spinoza, and to expel him from the people of Israel under the following anathema. According to the judgment of angels and of

* According to Boullainvilliers it was Morteira himself.

saints, we, with the full approval of the spiritual tribunal, and with the consent of every holy community, in the presence of the holy Books, with the six hundred and thirteen precepts therein contained, banish, expel, condemn, and curse Baruch Spinoza, with the curse which Joshua pronounced over Jericho, with the curse wherewith Elisha cursed the children, with all the curses which are written in the Book of the Law. Let him be cursed by day and cursed by night. Let him be cursed when he sleeps, and cursed when he rises up. Let him be cursed in his going out, and cursed in his coming in. May the Lord never forgive him. May the Lord cause his anger and jealousy against this man to burn, and visit him with all the curses that are written in the Book of the Law. Let his name be destroyed under heaven, and let him be separated to his destruction from all the tribes of Israel, with everything that is cursed in the Book of the Law. But you, who hold to the Lord your God, we greet you this day. See to it that no one of you address him, either by word of mouth or in writing, let no one of you show him any kindness, let no one of you be under the same roof with him, let no one remain standing within four yards' distance from him, let no one read anything that he has composed or written."

Spinoza was absent when the synagogue pronounced these denunciations upon him. He received the judgment in writing, and answered it by a protest in Spanish, which has unfortunately been lost to us. Further than this, he left the thing as it was. He was absorbed in his own thoughts, and troubled himself little about the anathema of a faith which had become quite worthless to him. What were the Rabbis to him compared with Descartes? In him he had found the teacher whom

his soul, in its instinctive desire for truth, needed. He
ceased henceforth to be a Jew, and exchanged his Jewish
name of Baruch for its Latin equivalent Benedictus, by
which name he calls himself in his letters and writings.

4. *His Life in Seclusion.*

Places of Abode.

If the narrative from which Boullainvilliers derived
his information is to be trusted, the excitement in the
Jewish community was not at all allayed after Spinoza's
excommunication, and in particular the Rabbis' thirst
for vengeance was not satisfied. Morteira above all
could not satisfy himself even by the extremest measures
of persecution against the apostate disciple. It is said
that along with the Christian clergy, who saw in Spinoza
a blasphemer, and who sympathized with the hatred of
the Rabbis, Morteira induced the magistrates of Amsterdam to banish Spinoza for some months from the town,
for the maintenance of order and of authority. Colerus
knows nothing of this. The thing is altogether little
worthy of belief, because at the time of the excommunication Spinoza had already left Amsterdam.

From this time forward he lived in the deepest
seclusion. During the following years—1656-1661—he
lived near Amsterdam, in a remote little villa, on the
way to Ouderkerk, where he found shelter under the
hospitable roof of a friend. This friend belonged to the
oppressed Protestants in the Netherlands, the Arminians
or Remonstrants, whom the Synod of Dort had condemned. As is well known, the theological and clerical
opponents of the Arminians were also enemies to
Descartes and his school. A second Synod of Dort had
condemned Cartesianism in the same year that the Jews

had thrust out Spinoza. The persecuted Jew found a refuge with the persecuted Christian. Many Arminians had emigrated, those who remained in the Netherlands formed a quiet community without clergy. They named themselves Collegiants, and had their head-quarters at Rhynsburg, near Leyden, for which reason they were also called the "Rhynsburgers;" they afterwards joined the Mennonites, who held Arminian views. Spinoza could feel himself in sympathy with the religious views of these people, who without any kind of ecclesiastical compulsion practised a severe purity of morals. Theirs was the only religious sect with which he still came in contact, and where the curse of his former co-religionists found no echo. Those writings and letters—which have lately been published by Van Vloten—were discovered in the Orphan Asylum of the Collegiants at Amsterdam.

Perhaps the sympathy, which Spinoza felt for their quiet community, was partly the reason why he accompanied his host to Rhynsburg, and stayed with him during the following years.* In May, 1664, he went to Voorburg, near the Hague, where he lived in the house of the artist Daniel Tydeman until 1669. After that, yielding to the request of his friends, he settled at the Hague altogether. At first he boarded on the Veerkay, with the widow Van Velden, inhabiting a small room on the second flat, quite at the end of the back building. In the same room Colerus lived afterwards, and wrote his biography of Spinoza. For the ·sake of a greater economy than was possible in the pension, Spinoza

* Colerus is mistaken in saying that Spinoza came to Rhyns-burg in the year 1664, and stayed there only one winter. It is certain that Oldenburg visited him there in the year 1661. Epist. i.

moved, in 1671, to the house of the artist Van der Spyck, where he managed his little housekeeping himself. There he remained until his death.

Let us now return to the history of the philosopher's mind, which we have already traced so far as it had its course in Judaism.

VIII.

Spinoza's Philosophical and Latin Education.

1. *The Study of Descartes.*

We cannot precisely fix the time when Spinoza became acquainted with the works of Descartes. It is certain that during his sojourn at Rhynsburg, he had already gone beyond his master, and was occupied with the chief work of his own philosophy. As early as 1661, at the commencement of his stay at Rhynsburg, he sent to his friend in London, Heinrich Oldenburg, a fragment of the *Ethics*, and two years later we find Simon Vries, one of his younger friends in Amsterdam, reading the *Ethics* in manuscript.*

Taking for granted—what is perfectly obvious—that several years were necessary for the study and comprehension of Descartes, and for the attainment and development of a higher standpoint for himself, we shall not go back too far, if we assign the beginning of his Cartesian studies to the last part of his Rabbinical life, and place it before his separation from the synagogue. Mere doubts which had arisen within him could not have given him such a firm and immovable demeanour as he maintained in opposition to the Rabbis, when he thwarted their attempt for his conversion, rejected their promises,

* Epist. ii. (to Oldenburg) Epist. xxvi. (from Simon Vries),

and quietly accepted and endured their threats and
curses. He was no wavering reed like Uriel Acosta.
His doubts had a sufficient ground and were not to be
overthrown, and his convictions were certain, when he
renounced Judaism. Even then his brain was filled and
enlightened with the ideas of Descartes. The world
within him was clear, and he need not let it disturb him,
if the dark world without hurled its lightnings after him.

2. *The Latin Language.*

The study of Descartes, and especially that of his two
fundamental works—the *Meditations* and the *Principles*
—presupposes a knowledge of the Latin language.
Spinoza must have understood it already, when he could
easily and quickly read through the chief writings of
Descartes. To be able himself to become a teacher of
philosophy to his age and to the world, he must have
appropriated it as a second mother tongue. He obtained
the mastery over this language to an astonishing degree.
His Latinity is indeed so clear and so transparent, so
constantly adequate and adapted to the meaning, so
firm and certain in its style, that it can be called in its
own way classical, using this word in the only sense
which is justifiable.

If, then, his Cartesian studies are to be reckoned
among the motives which led to his rupture with Judaism
and the synagogue, we are obliged to suppose that his
Latin studies preceded that event. In his fifteenth year
he was a finished Talmudist. Hitherto his education had
been entirely Jewish. He was in his twenty-fourth year
when the synagogue excommunicated him, and by that
time his mind was already entirely possessed by the
teaching of Descartes. His Latin education, received of

course outside the Rabbinical school, must be assigned
to this interval. He learned languages easily, and neither
his knowledge of nor his practice in foreign idioms was
small. Of modern languages he knew Portuguese, Spanish,
Italian, French, Dutch, German. Then, in addition to
all these and Latin, he had an excellent knowledge of
Hebrew; he even drew up a Hebrew grammar on a new
method.

His interest in Latin led him to the school of a man
who not only furthered his Latin culture, but also did
something to fix the direction of his mental development.
This intercourse fostered Spinoza's aversion to Judaism,
and he may have been the first who introduced Spinoza
to philosophy and Descartes.

IX.

INTERCOURSE WITH VAN DEN ENDE.

1. *Franz Van den Ende.*

Spinoza received his first Latin lesson from a German
whose name is not known. His higher Latin culture he
owed to the physician Franz Van den Ende, in Amsterdam,
who was known as a learned humanist, and who was
generally sought after as a teacher of philosophy. The
richest people in the city placed their sons under his
instruction. His love for the literature of classical
antiquity, in which he felt himself at home, together with
his studies as a physician in natural science, had entirely
estranged his mind from the dogmas of his Church. He
was a free-thinker, who influenced the minds of his
pupils not only by his classical culture, but also by his
rationalistic mode of thinking. His instructions fell

under suspicion, and at last, Colerus says, it was discovered that he sowed the seeds of Atheism in the minds of the young people intrusted to his care. "That," he adds, "is a fact, which if necessary I could prove by the testimony of several respectable people who are still alive. To this day these good souls bless their parents for taking them out of the hands of such a corrupt and godless teacher, and saving them in good time from the school of Satan."

From all this it is probable that, under the influence of this man, Spinoza not only perfected his Latin, but at the same time received an impulse towards the natural sciences, which led him to Descartes. Latin was the bridge between his Hebrew and Cartesian education, and it is in this part of his life that the influence of Van den Ende was important.*

The last years of this learned physician were adventurous and his end was very tragical. After having lost in

---

* Boullainvilliers relates that Van den Ende offered to take Spinoza into his house and to give him instruction on the condition that afterwards, when he had received the requisite culture, he should help him as assistant teacher. It can only have been after his rupture with the synagogue, when Spinoza needed such a refuge, that Van den Ende offered him the shelter of his house. This offer presupposes an intimate acquaintance between the two, which could not have existed until Spinoza had been sometime in Van den Ende's school. In any circumstances, his connection with the learned physician must have begun before his rupture with the synagogue, for at that time he no longer lived in Amsterdam. Neither can it have begun only a short time previously, for that would allow too brief an interval for his Latin education. Therefore in this respect also the narrative from which Boullainvilliers drew his information is uncertain and confused. It is impossible that when Van den Ende offered his house as an asylum to the excommunicated Spinoza he should then, for the first time, have also offered to give him instruction.

Holland, probably owing to his evil reputation as an atheist, both the esteem of the people and his means of livelihood, he went to France, where for some time he pursued his profession as a doctor, and at last ended his life on the gallows for a political crime (1672). There was a rumour that he had made an attempt on the life of the Dauphin. He had, in fact, taken part in a political conspiracy, the object of which was to bring about a rising in Normandy and Bretagne, and to hand them over to Holland. Rohan and La Truaumont stood at the head of the plot and used, De la Fare tells us in his *Memoirs,* "a Dutch schoolmaster" as their tool. What interested Van den Ende in this scheme was his patriotic desire to occupy the King of France, who was then at war with the Netherlands, by creating a disturbance in his own kingdom.

2. *Clara Maria Van den Ende.*

Besides the education and the incitements to study which Spinoza found in his master's house, there was another attraction which appealed to his heart. Van den Ende had an only daughter, Clara Maria, who took part in her father's learned studies. She knew Latin so well, that in the absence of her father, she could teach his pupils. She was not beautiful, but clever, capable, of a cheerful disposition and skilled in music, and these charms won Spinoza's love. He himself subsequently often acknowledged that he loved her and that he intended to marry her.

Another of Van den Ende's pupils called Kerckrinck was Spinoza's rival, and he carried off the prize with the aid of a necklace which he presented to his instructress. She became Kerckrinck's wife, he having by that time gone over to the Catholic Church. So Colerus tells the story, referring to Bayle and Sebastian Kortholt. The latter does not speak of any love affair of Spinoza, and only tells us that he was taught Latin by a girl along with Kerckrinck from Hamburg, who afterwards married the teacher. However, Colerus does not exactly say that Spinoza was her pupil, only that he had frequent opportunities of seeing and of conversing with her, and so conceived an affection for her. This certainly seems as if Colerus too connected their intimacy with the lessons of Spinoza.

The chronological facts recently brought to light by Van Vloten from the marriage register in Amsterdam, destroy part of this narrative. The marriage between Dirck Kerckrinck and Clara Maria Van den Ende took place on the 5th of February, 1671, when Kerckrinck was thirty-two years of age and his bride was twenty-seven. At the time of Spinoza's excommunication Clara was twelve years old, after that Van den Ende cannot any longer have been his teacher, and therefore it is impossible that his daughter can ever have given him any lessons. It is even difficult to assign any date for Spinoza's love. While he lived in Amsterdam the daughter of Van den Ende was a child; when he left the neighbourhood of Amsterdam altogether she was only sixteen. But since Spinoza himself, according to Colerus, whom there is every reason to believe, often spoke of his love, we must suppose that after the excommunication and his removal from Amsterdam, he still maintained some intercourse with the family of Van den Ende for a considerable time, by means of visits. From that country house between Amsterdam and Ouderkerk it was easy to hold intercourse with his friends, and during the years from 1656-1660, when he stayed in that house he must have come often to the town. We also know from his letters that he travelled to Amsterdam from Rhynsburg, and remained there for weeks. He did so in the autumn of 1661, in April, 1663, in the end of March, 1665.* During these years, this affection must have seriously taken possession of Spinoza, and led him to think of a union with the daughter of his teacher. Yet it is strange that the name of Van den Ende is never mentioned in his letters.

The happiness of this love, if indeed Spinoza was ever passionately absorbed by it, was a transient dream, soon followed by a final renunciation. Such renunciation was no hard fate for a man of Spinoza's temper, it was of a piece with the mood which was dominant and lasting within him. In one of such a temper the passions have no stormy and overwhelming dominion. The love and the renunciation of Spinoza must not be imagined after the manner of ordinary sentimental emotions. With the pangs of love such a head could not have much to do. It was too clear to be darkened by passion. Therefore this love is not a happy or suggestive theme for a romance. If a touching story of the heart is to be made out of it, Spinoza's head must be forgotten, and how much of Spinoza is left then for the romance?

X.

Spinoza's Character and Mode of Living.

1. *Independence and Solitude.*

The expedients which Spinoza's enemies could devise against him were exhausted. They had tried successively bribery, assassination, excommunication and banishment.

* Epist. iv. and ix. (to Oldenburg) ; Ep. xxxviii. (to Blyenbergh).

8

This last he was obliged voluntarily to choose, otherwise an edict for the purpose would have been formally pronounced. Never was an independent life more hardly fought for, never was it lived out more purely and quietly than in this instance, in which a man was obliged to break with his parents, his church, his faith, and with the enjoyments of life, in order to live for his thoughts, and in which he accepted and bore this destiny so that his peace of mind did not suffer from it.

His ancestral religion rejected him, and he rejected it. He joined himself to no other faith. He belonged no more to any of the religions having a position in the world, not even in outward appearance, for he despised appearances. He had forsaken those foundations on which human communities are based ; he had torn himself away as it were from the band of human society. He was entirely independent, and entirely alone. This independence and solitude, wrung from fate with inflexible perseverance, he guarded to his last breath. They were his only and his greatest possession; they were the mode of life in which his soul felt at ease, they were the simple and genuine expression of his character.

2. *His means of livelihood.*

This character was so firmly and distinctly impressed even on the smallest incidents of his external life, that its simplicity and purity are recognized in everything.

A first condition of his independence was to gain a livelihood for himself. For what avails all spiritual freedom when one cannot exist without the help of others. A wise ordinance of the *Talmud* obliges every Jewish scholar to learn, in addition to intellectual knowledge, a trade or mechanical art, in the exercise of which he may recruit himself from mental labours. Since the mind cannot always be active, some such secondary occupation seemed to the Talmudists to be specially necessary, in order to leave no room for idleness, the source of evil habits. Certainly Spinoza did not need for such a reason to comply with the injunctions of the *Talmud.* He required along with Philosophy—which was his real and true vocation—some occupation to support him ; and he knew how to combine this business with his studies in mathematics, and natural science. He learned the art of grinding lenses, an art with which we know that Descartes also occupied himself much and zealously, during the course of his preliminary studies for his *Dioptrics.**

Colerus tells us, that Spinoza was said to have been so skilful an optician, that his glasses were everywhere sought after. Many of these glasses which he left behind at his death were sold at a good price.

He was besides an amateur painter, and is said to have liked to try his hand at portrait painting, although not of course with a view to make money by it. Colerus saw a collection of such drawings, a kind of album in which Spinoza had drawn persons of his acquaintance, and amongst others himself, apparently as Masaniello. He must have been in a cheerful humour, when he jestingly represented his own features in the picture of the Neapolitan fisherman.

3. *Unselfishness.*

It is impossible to be selfish and independent at the same time. For selfishness is eager for gain, and loves

* See my *History of Modern Philosophy* (second edition). First volume, part i. First book, chap. v., pp. 167, 168.

profit best, when it comes as a gift without trouble. To the egotist nothing is easier than to accept and to live at the expense of others, and thus obligations are necessarily incurred by the receiver by which his independence is compromised. Even if no obligations are connected with these benefactions and favours, a man loses in his own eyes the firm and certain consciousness of an independent existence. Therefore a fine sense of one's own independence is shy of accepting favours. I do not by this mean to say that Spinoza's perfect unselfishness was merely for the sake of his independence, but it helped to further it, and it was rooted in his own nature, which desired none of the things which are of importance to human selfishness.

Even the well meant offers of his friends he was accustomed to decline. One of his truest friends and pupils, Simon Vries, in Amsterdam, offered him a present of two thousand florins, which Spinoza refused, because he had no use for it, and the possession would as he said be burdensome to him. When Simon Vries was dying, he wished, since he was unmarried and childless, to make his friend the sole heir of his property. Spinoza rejected this inheritance, and begged Simon Vries to bequeath it to his own brother. Even the small annuity which he was to receive from this brother he reduced to a smaller sum than was proposed.

His sisters disputed with him his portion of the paternal inheritance. He caused his claim to be decided by a lawsuit, which confirmed it; but he then voluntarily gave up his share to them. A friend once finding him shabbily dressed, begged him to accept a better garment. Spinoza thanked him, saying : What is the use of a costly covering for a worthless thing ?

4. *Freedom from Wants.*

He earned as much as he required. More he did not wish, and he needed very little. There is nothing more conducive to outward independence, than freedom from wants. This virtue Spinoza possessed in the highest degree. In this respect he reminds us of the examples of noble simplicity among the philosophers of antiquity. It has been estimated that his daily necessities cost about twopence ! He was very economical.

The small housekeeping which, during his last years, he managed himself, was scrupulously arranged. The little bills, which ran up for three months, were punctually paid on the day they were due. His dress also was poor, and was neglected rather than considered. He who wishes to be without cares must have few needs. Spinoza had reduced his life to the smallest scale of human wants, and thus he was able to devote himself entirely to the knowledge of truth. What he wanted to spare himself was not money, but wants and cares, which engross the mind and bring it to a miserable state. His mode of life was the right one for preserving quietness of soul, and for coming to terms with the world in the shortest way.

5. *Domestic Life.*

In his intercourse with the people living in the house with him he was kind and gentle, sympathizing with their interests, never burdensome to anyone, and mild and peaceable in his conversation. Thus he liked sometimes to talk over with his companions the Sunday's sermon which they had heard. "The chief thing in religion," he said, "is a pious, quiet, and peaceful life." He would

come back to this sentence, and as for the rest he left the
religious views of others undisturbed.

I will give a little picture of his domestic life in the
words of Colerus : " He remained the greater part of the
day quietly in his room. Sometimes when he felt tired
with his deep meditations he came down stairs, to refresh
himself, and talked with the people of the house, even
about trifles. Now and then he enjoyed a pipe ; or, if he
wished a longer recreation, he caught spiders which fought
with each other, or flies which he threw into a spider's
net, and then watched the struggles of the two animals
with so much amusement that sometimes he laughed
aloud. He also observed under the microscope the
organization of the smallest insects, and drew conclusions
from these, which were of use to him in his physical
studies."

6. *The Call to Heidelberg.*

As he kept his poverty in preference to the inheritance
of his rich friend, he also remained true to his solitary life,
when a few years before his death he received an honourable call to public philosophical activity.

The Elector of the Palatinate, Charles Louis, the brother
of that interesting and learned princess to whom Descartes
dedicated his chief work, wished to secure Spinoza for
his university at Heidelberg. He offered the chair of
philosophy in Heidelberg to the philosopher of the
Hague, and sent the proposal through Professor Fabricius
with expressions of the greatest admiration. Fabricius
wrote on the 16th of February, 1673, to Spinoza : " His
Grace the Elector of the Palatinate, my gracious sovereign,
has commanded me to write to you, since you, although
unknown to me, have been strongly recommended to his
Grace, and to ask if you are inclined to accept a regular

chair of philosophy at his celebrated university. You will receive the salary of a regular Professor. Nowhere could you find a sovereign more favourably disposed to men of genius, among whom he counts you. You will moreover have entire freedom in your philosophical labours, which freedom the prince is assured will not be misused by you to the disturbance of the established religion. I only add : If you come hither you will enjoy a true philosophical life, unless everything should turn out differently from what we hope and expect."

Things did in fact turn out differently; for Spinoza declined the call. He answered on the 30th of March, 1673 : "If I ever cherished the wish to undertake an academic chair, I could not have desired any better appointment than that which his Grace the Elector of the Palatinate offers me through you, especially on account of the freedom in philosophical study which the prince undertakes to grant me; not to speak of the desire I have long had to live under the government of such a prince whose wisdom is admired by the world. However, since I never felt an inclination to teach in public, I cannot make up my mind to avail myself of this excellent opportunity, though I have well considered the matter.

"My first objection is that I should not be able to continue my own studies in philosophy, if my time were dedicated to the instruction of the youth of the university. Next, I do not know where the limits of the philosophical freedom spoken of are to be drawn, so that it may not be said that I am seeking to disturb the established religion. For discord does not spring from eager enthusiasm for the cause of religion, but from the manifold passions and the quarrelsome zeal of people, who have a way of contradicting and condemning everything, not excepting even

what is perfectly correct. In my quiet lonely life I have
already experienced those difficulties, and I certainly
should have to expect them in a larger measure in such
a public position. It is not, you perceive, the hope of
any better outward lot that keeps me back, but my love
for that quietness, which I hope to be able to preserve to
some extent if I abstain from all public teaching."*

7. *Fearlessness.*

One emotion was quite unknown to him, the fear of
death, that greatest enemy of peace in the soul of man.
And since *this* fear never troubled him he was altogether
fearless. His moral courage was so strong and firm,
that although delicate and worn out by illness, he did
not shrink from dangers, which would have deprived
most people of all presence of mind. Of this he gave an
extraordinary example, which Van der Spyck witnessed
and reported to Colerus. One would not have thought
that Spinoza, who lived so quietly and so far removed
from all worldly affairs, would ever have been exposed
to a bloodthirsty mob. But the mob is ever the same,
a wild herd of blind passions. It was during the time of
the war between France and the Netherlands, which
embittered all hearts in Holland against the republican
party, and all who were supposed to be friends of the
French. The title of a "friend of France" sufficed to
cause a man to be stoned to death. In August, 1672,
the mob at the Hague had torn to pieces the brothers
Witt, who were the heads of the Republicans. In the
following year the colonel of a French regiment in
Utrecht, called Stoupe, who was interested in Spinoza,
and especially in his "theologico-political treatise,"

* Epist. liv.

which had just appeared, invited the philosopher to come
to Utrecht to make the acquaintance of the Prince de
Condé. When Spinoza returned from this journey the
rumour had spread at the Hague that he was a French
spy, who carried on a secret and treacherous negotiation
with the enemy of the country. Already the terrorists
were heard to say that he must be put to death. His
landlord, Van der Spyck, was in the greatest anxiety lest
his house should be stormed by the mob. The only one
who remained calm and consoled him was Spinoza:
" Fear nothing," he said, " as soon as the smallest noise
is heard at your door I shall go out and walk straight
among the people, even should I meet with the same
fate as the poor brothers Witt. I am a good republican,
and never have wished anything but the glory and
advantage of the State."

8. *Seriousness and Melancholy.*

Condemnation of Hypocrisy.

The essence and the occupation of his life was solitary
and profound meditation. The independence of his mind
showed itself in this, that he occupied himself far more
with his own thoughts than with the thoughts of others,
and for this reason he read little. When he could be
alone in the quietness of his study with his thoughts
Spinoza was quite himself. There he was free and happy.
Solitude belonged to his nature. Often he remained for
days together without seeing anybody, and without ever
leaving his room. His philosophical works were chiefly
written at night. The spirit of the doctrine of this man
was completely embodied in himself. He had freed
himself entirely from desires and passions, because he
had completely seen through them. Thus he was entirely

master of himself, always undisturbed in the serenity of
his spirit, overpowered by no impulse of emotion, and so
he was never extravagant either in joy or in sorrow.

There is a depth of insight which is not compatible
with the mere enjoyment of life, because the gay glitter
of the world cannot dazzle this insight any more. *Nur
der Irrthum ist das Leben.* Real and penetrating
observers of human nature, to the very small number of
whom Spinoza belonged, easily acquire a melancholy,
which is neither sad nor gloomy. Their minds are too
clear to become darkened, but they cannot help contem-
plating the common pleasures of the world and of life as
a thing far beneath them, and as a hurrying scene of
strange confusion. Hence arises the irresistible desire
for solitude, which is inevitably bound up in characters
of this stamp, and forms one of their most essential
features. He who really sees through human nature
likes it best in its simplest and plainest forms, and is not
angry with its errors and delusions. There is only one
case in which such a man finds it difficult to refrain from
utter condemnation, and that is when there is intentional
deceit, when the life, hollow in reality, puts on a false
appearance, when it ceases to be genuine and plays the
hypocrite, as if the observer of human nature did not see
through it. Every kind of hypocrisy, under whatever
form it veils itself, is to the student of human nature
simply an insolence. And to the insolence of falsehood
Spinoza was always relentless. This repugnance sprang
from his very truthfulness, he never wished to master it,
for to do so would have been contrary to his nature.
His language becomes incisive and harsh, when it is
called forth by this kind of falsehood. His letter to
Albert Burgh was written in this strain. Burgh was a

former pupil of Spinoza, who had been converted to Catholicism in Italy, and dared to try to convert Spinoza, by addressing a letter to him in the style of a clumsy pulpit admonition.* And I can imagine that when Spinoza, in his dealings with the Rabbis, twenty years earlier, had been challenged by them, and—convinced in himself of the essential falseness of theological and talmudical Judaism—took such a decisive attitude of repellent rebuke, there was nothing left to the men of the synagogue but to excommunicate him.

XI.

Spinoza's Death.

1. *His Quiet End.*

As Spinoza lived, so he died; quietly and peacefully, and free from all the fears and terrors of death. In him that renunciation which death forces upon us, and which is so difficult to human weakness and love of life, had long been gladly and voluntarily accomplished. If dying to the world consists in this renunciation, in this turning away from the enjoyment, and from those desires which cling "with clasping hands" to the earth, then this condition was well known and familiar to our philosopher. His life was that which Socrates declares death to be; and, like Socrates, he met his last hours with his usual calm and unmoved bearing.

For more than twenty years he had suffered from his chest, and his bodily appearance bore the undoubted impress of consumption. But he never spoke of his sufferings to others, and never complained; he would

* Epist. lxxiii., lxxiv.

not receive help from others lest he should be burdensome to anyone.   Even the people who lived in the same
house with him never suspected how rapidly death was
approaching.   He had come down, as he generally did in
the evening, and talked for a long time with his companions about the sermon which they had just heard.
That evening he went to bed earlier than usual.   The
next day, Sunday, February 23rd, 1677, he came once
more down stairs, before Church-time to speak with his
friends.   In the meantime Dr. Ludwig Meyer, of Amsterdam, to whom Spinoza had written, arrived.   He gave
his suffering friend such medical assistance as he could ;
and, amongst other orders, desired the landlady to kill a
chicken, that Spinoza might have some soup for dinner.
This was done, and Spinoza ate the soup with a good
appetite.   When Van der Spyck and his wife returned
from the afternoon service, they heard that Spinoza had
died about three o'clock.   Nobody was with him in his
last hours except the doctor from Amsterdam, who went
away again the same evening.

Such is the account of Spinoza's death that the people
of the house more than once related to Colerus, assuring
him that all other reports of it were nothing but lies.

2. *False Reports.*

The story of Menagius, that Spinoza had gone to
France, had been there threatened with the Bastille by
the fanatical zeal of the Minister Pomponne, that there-
upon he had fled in the disguise of a Franciscan friar,
and had died, after his return, from the terror of the
Bastille—these lies I only mention as a specimen of the
falsehoods, which were current.   They are derived from
the source from which Menagius also drew when he said

that Spinoza carried on his brow the sign of reprobation. This sign rather rests upon the lying forehead of the *Menagiana*.*

Although Spinoza did not die from fear, others spread the report that he died in fear, and distress of mind, and that he repeatedly sighed, and exclaimed: " God have mercy upon me, and be gracious to me, a miserable sinner ! " If this were true, such an expression of anguish is but human. Who is sure of what he will be in his last hours ? Lessing himself said, when the theologians with whom he was arguing, reminded him, almost threateningly, of the last anguish of conscience : " I shall perhaps tremble in my last hour, but I shall not tremble at the thought of it." These reports, however, are not true ; and Colerus, whose interest would not be to deny them, declares them to be lies. No one knows what the last hours of Spinoza were ; no one was beside him but a friend who said nothing about it. Spinoza's death could not be worse than his long sufferings. Yet the decided testimony of those who lived for years in daily intercourse with him is that they never heard him utter a sound of complaint.

Another report, which Colerus contradicts, declares that Spinoza, when he felt that death was drawing near, stupified himself with mandragora juice to alleviate his last moments. This was at last magnified into an accusation of suicide. A confused paragraph in the biography of Lucas perhaps helped to give currency to this report. " Our philosopher," so runs the passage, " is not only to be called happy for the fame of his virtue, but also on account of the circumstances of his death, which he met quite fearlessly, as we know from those who were with

* *Menagiana.* Amst. 1695.

him. He willingly sacrified himself for his enemies that
their conscience might not be stained with his murder."
From this it might appear that Spinoza had avoided
persecution by a voluntary death, not for his own sake,
but to save his enemies from crime. What a silly inven-
tion! When a man suffers for twenty years and more
from consumption, he has no need of suicide in order to
die. And if Spinoza wished to die either from love or
hatred of his persecutors, he ought to have died twenty
years earlier. But all the reports show how his enemies,
as well as his admirers were unable to discern the greatness of his soul. The one makes of him a miserable
coward, the others a crack-brained martyr.

XII.

SPINOZA'S OUTWARD APPEARANCE.

Colerus asked a great many persons at the Hague, who
had seen and known Spinoza, to describe his appearance.
" He was of a middle size, with regular and well-formed
features, a rather sallow complexion, black curly hair,
and long black eyebrows : he could be recognized at
once as a Portuguese Jew." Leibnitz also, who visited
him at the Hague a year before his death, describes his
looks in similar terms : "The celebrated Jew Spinoza
had an olive complexion, and something Spanish in his
face."

His continuous and wasting illness left traces of suffering on his countenance; but what is most striking in it
is the habit of thought, shown in his noble forehead and
in his earnest look. "He carried the sign of rejection
on his forehead!" Such is the interpretation which a
blind hatred gives to this feature.

"It is the sombre expression of a deep thinker." Such is the interpretation of a German philosopher who better understands the characteristics of a Spinoza. A sign of rejection it certainly was, but rejection not passive, but active. The philosopher rejects the errors, the thoughtless passions, and above all, the falsehood of men!

III.

SPINOZA:

THE (GLAD) HERALD TO MANKIND OF THE GOOD NEWS OF ITS MAJORITY;

AN ORATION

DELIVERED ON THE OCCASION OF THE UNVEILING OF
THE STATUE AT THE HAGUE, SEPT. 18TH, 1880,

BY

DR. J. VAN VLOTEN.

TRANSLATED BY

THE REV. ALLAN MENZIES,

CLASSICAL EXAMINER TO THE UNIVERSITY OF ST. ANDREWS.

9

SPINOZA;

An Oration delivered at the Unveiling of his Statue.

"Spit on that grave—there lies Spinoza." These words were used more than a century and a half ago by Karel Tuinman, minister at Middelburg, of the then predominant Reformed Church—a divine surely, fuller of faith than love. And now, a few steps from that grave, stands the statue, in a few minutes to be unveiled, of the man with regard to whom this courteous invitation was spoken; while over it there wave the banners of all those countries of the Old World and of the New, from which contributions have poured into our hands, to help in its erection, from Moscow to New York, from Java to the Argentine Republic. When I see all this display of flags, and the crowd which has assembled on this spot, I turn to the modest dwelling there beside us, where the philosopher spent his last years, and I imagine that I see him, in the simple dress he wore in the house, appear at the window among those with whom he lived, to ask what it is all about, and hearing that it all had reference to him and his memory, shyly draw back again into the room. It is not for his sake, indeed, that all this display is made to-day, and that his statue is henceforward to look down from this place. It is for the sake of those who reverence his memory, and to impress more deeply upon every one how great is the significance to civilized

9 *

humanity of the man, who is here represented as he wa
during his lifetime. But how shall we explain the
mighty difference between the estimate of that age, and
the estimate of this ; between the Rev. Mr. Tuinman,
who detested and execrated him, and the large number
of our contemporaries who now pay him homage, for I
would not undertake to say that there are not some still
living who share that worthy's prejudice and hatred. But
a great change has undoubtedly taken place : how is it
to be accounted for ? It arises from the nature of the
case, from the ordinary course of events, from the
conflict—never to be avoided—between the spirit of the
increasing future, and that of the past, as it grows old
and obsolete. The past ever dreads and condemns,
suspects and execrates the future, by which it is being
insensibly replaced ; and this repugnance will find
expression in proportion to the civilization reached by its
prejudiced representatives. A hundred and fifty years
before Mr. Tuinman's day, those whose belief he inherited
carried on the Dutch Protestants'—the Beggars'—revolt
against Rome and Spain ; they then represented the
future, and suffered martyrdom and the fire at the hands
of the passionate adherents of the past. Thus the
objects of the man's ecclesiastical hatred might, in a
certain sense, count themselves fortunate that he did not
carry things so far, but contented himself with the
unseemly exhortation to spitting. That future, which
was persecuted in Spinoza, now promises more and more
to become the present ; that faith which parts company
with love and sits in judgment on mankind, is about to
yield to a reasonable and loving intelligence, which tends
to make men brethren ; and our presence on this spot,
the unveiling of this statue for which we have come

together, is an expressive symbol of this cheering alteration of the times.

There is certainly some appropriateness in the fact that it was in this land of sturdy Protestants—in the country of those men who, in their thorough going opposition to the tyranny of Pope and King, gave to Europe by their bold and unsupported abjuration of an autocratic sovereign the example of an independent free Republic—that the thinker was born, though of a foreign race, who, as he always attached the greatest value to the privilege he thus possessed, was inspired and aided by the free atmosphere he breathed, to work out his philosophy of life, and thus complete the civilizing work of a Reformation which had come to a halt half way in its career. For this, it is more and more coming to be recognized, is the true significance of the man, whose memory we are here to celebrate to-day.

What, let us ask, is the principle of the Reformation? It is that man possesses an inalienable right to his moral and intellectual development. It was to maintain this right against a tyrannical Sovereign and Pontiff, who sought to cast over them the bonds of their narrow and selfish theories of Church and State, that the Beggars put forth those noble efforts which were crowned with such brilliant success. In this they naturally did not transcend the views they had attained of Church polity and of doctrine. But had they bound themselves for all time coming to the views which they then held, or if—feeling no lofty intellectual and moral needs themselves—they had sought to make these views binding in all time coming upon others, they would have shown the same want of understanding of man's nature and destiny, as that which they had so successfully combated in the

golden age of Protestantism, when face to face with Rome
and Spain.   And in Spinoza, born and brought up as he
was on Protestant ground—the son of a Jewish family
but rejected by his own people—there was afterwards
manifested, with equal power and equal thoroughness, that
same Reformation principle.   That the Protestants of his
day should recognize this was not to be expected; his
witness was borne in a land where the beneficent influence
of the Reformation had come to a standstill, and in the
face of the blind clamour of its prejudiced preachers,
such as Tuinman, and his kind.

There are at all times, unfortunately, a number of
individuals to be found, who, though arrived at full
physical development and come to years of maturity, yet
in the sphere of the intellect and of morals, are either
without their due share of ability to enable them to think
for themselves, or influenced by a pitiable love of ease, so
that they neither dare nor desire to walk by themselves,
without leaning on the crutches which are offered to them
by apparently well-meaning people.   We also observe
that there are persons to be found who do not scruple to
take advantage of their weakness, and to sell as dearly as
they can the aid and support of which their neighbours
stand in need.   But this man, whose humble but useful
handicraft led him to add artificial strength to his
fellow-citizens' bodily eyes, made it his business to teach
men, for no fee or reward, and with the best results for
those who took up the easy yoke of being his disciples,
to walk in the world of thought without crutches, and to
look about them with their own unaided eyes.

How did he set about this task ?   He simply directed
men to that part of their nature, which, though so often
unvalued and miserably neglected, is yet, when man is

most civilized, his true patent of nobility—his *reason*.
He had good cause to be persuaded, that when not based
on reason as its indispensable support, the imagination of
man's heart was too likely to be evil. He had his own
experience to look back upon, when the synagogue had
rudely thrust him out; and he could call up to his mind
that infamous Saturday evening of August, 1672, when a
Christian population, that deemed itself "Reformed,"
diligently stirred up by its preachers of the Gospel, and
now inflamed and led on by some of its rulers, barbarously
murdered the Grand Pensionary of Holland and his
brother. Whence came then the undeniable tendency to
evil of the human heart? Solely from the irrational
suggestions of his passions, which degrade him from a
reasonable and moral being, acting for his own welfare
and that of others, to a tool and victim of impulses
neither reasonable nor moral; from a noble "actor" to a
pitiable "sufferer." Suffering is the right name to apply
to every emotion or impulse which makes a man no longer
master of himself, closes his ear to the voice of his better
self, and drives him to the commission of the most
unreasonable actions.

In reason, on the contrary—which is the highest
expression of human civilization as nature intended it
to be—all may count themselves one, and love takes
the place of hatred as the ruling motive and pivot of
society. Thus there flows from its beneficent action no
harsh benumbing alienation from the world and its affairs.
On the contrary, this thinker, who was entitled to take
for his motto that "true wisdom is not a contemplation of
death, but a contemplation of life," knew how to estimate
human life when governed by reason, at its true worth, to
assign to it its fullest value. A phrase he used, "doing

good and being glad," appears simple enough, but is
seen, when we consider the inseparable connection of the
two things, to be full of meaning. It may be interpreted
by his other phrase, that "active virtue is enjoyment;"
and is, in fact, a short and compendious expression of the
essence.of his whole ethical teaching. So far was he
removed from that ill-natured depreciation of men and
things, which constitutes the sickly distinction of some
of the geniuses of our days. They, and their numerous
imitators, led astray by false reasoning, and giving
themselves up to unbalanced contemplation of all the
evil they have so carefully studied, lose their capacity to
perceive the good, which presents itself as really as the
evil to the observation of every one who is not wilfully
blind to it, and which they ought to gird themselves up
to foster and increase, instead of filling street and market
with their weak lamentations. Spinoza was no Optimist,
as it is called; he had no share at least in that con-
temptible and mischievous optimism which is at peace
with everything, even with what is least praiseworthy,
and can palliate and excuse even what is most repulsive;
but he certainly was an Anti-pessimist. Such an one
apprehends that there is in the world much that is good
and beautiful, much that is noble and exalted, both
handed down to us from the past, and waiting to be
realized by our endeavours; and that the true happiness
of each man consists in contributing to this great end,
in proportion to the measure of his powers, and according
to the place in life which he has chosen, or fortune has
assigned him. A more exalted feeling of life, consciousness of life, need of life, must be the result, equally
beneficent and welcome, of such an attitude of mind;
and this must lead to the most sympathetic activity.

" Pleasure, joy, active interest in things," as Goethe once exclaimed in the spirit of Spinoza, " this only is essential —all else is frivolity and vanity." If we were seeking to sum up in one short phrase the marrow of Spinoza's thought as bearing on morals and society, the phrase we should employ would be " unquenchable energy of reason and love."

So far from the truth is that senseless misapprehension which has too often been heard to declare that Spinoza's teaching encourages a purely passive inactivity in practice. Such an incorrect impression can be put down to nothing but the sheerest shortsightedness and superficiality. To no other qualities could it be possible so to judge one, who exhibited the finest feeling, the keenest insight into the motives of human action throughout all their shades and varieties, and to make him a sort of Eastern dreamer, to whom all things without distinction were obliterated in the mist of an all-embracing Deity. How otherwise could writers like Saisset have failed to see in him the bold thinker, who, unlike the prophets of lamentation and death, summons men to life, to live themselves and to make others live, who tells them that they are not called to mope and drudge, but to live and work ? how could they have decried him as the apostle of an aimless and fruitless philosophy, which by force of abstract musing had lost all sense for personal activity ? How could they have spoken of him as one, whose character was devoid of elasticity, and who in the pitiable cloister life he led, knew neither needs nor emotions ? How could it be said of him, as it is said even by a Kuno Fischer, that what he had before his eye was the connection of things, but not the things themselves ? as if he had never written his account of the origin of the human

passions, in which he displays such a knowledge of human
nature, or the delicate sketch of man's vain and unhappy
state, when he neglects his active vocation in life, and
gives himself passively over to the irrational whirlpool of
his emotional impressions ?   No, certainly; elevating,
life-awakening energy is always and everywhere the
unmistakable central aim of his work as a philosopher,
and in this cause he is even able to enlist every noble
emotion, transformed for the purpose from a passive and
irrational impulse to a reasonable and active principle. His
doctrine taught that all emotions, in the presence of which
the mind carries on the activity of thought, are signs of
moral strength, which may be divided into two kinds of
strength, " sagacity" and " generosity." Sagacity is
moral virtue in respect to that which chiefly concerns a
man's own interest, in the highest sense of the word;
generosity, where the interest of others is the aim in view.
From this point of view indeed the one kind of virtue
is inseparable from the other; no fancy can be more
mistaken than that a man's pursuit of his own good
in this way can be the root of all sorts of evil, and not
rather of virtue.   And the most startling characteristic of
Spinoza's acute and unhesitating exposition of man's
material and moral nature, in their indissoluble union with
each other, is just his consistent maintenance of a doctrine
which is so frequently and so gravely misunderstood.
The highest good of all is a social one, into which all may
enter and rejoice together, when—following the inborn
impulse of their human nature—they actively and un-
weariedly carry on the development of their rational
faculties.   The view of the infinite solidarity of all
things with each other, and the consciousness of each
man's necessary connection with all things—gradually

opened up, as we pursue this line of thought—this is common to all, this can be acquired by all. Out of this activity there springs a benevolent frame of mind, which is simply a form of that which, in its unpurified, ecclesiastical state is called religion, but is here purged of all misunderstanding, and justified to reason. This leads to a love, which is secure against those narrow hatreds that divide men of different creeds, and which is the social cement of the future for which all are longing. He who seeks to live in this spirit according to the dictates of reason, will be far removed from hating others, indeed he will seek to overcome their hatred, their wrath, their scorn, and everything of that kind by his own generous love. Hatred stirs up nothing but hatred : love, on the contrary, is able to quench hatred. " The man, who seeks to avenge the insult done to him by returning hatred, leads a miserable life ; but he who sets himself to drive away hatred by love, fights his battle happy and in security, resists with equal ease one antagonist or many, and requires as little as possible any external aid. Those whom he overcomes gladly relinquish to him the field, not because they feel that they are beaten, but because their forces are increased. Passions divide men, reason brings them together ; there is nothing more useful to men than a man who lets reason guide him."

This was well known to the genial poet, who wished

> " All men were wise,
> Then earth would be a paradise."

But the poet desired and yearned after such a result in vain : our thinker pointed out the way to it, and if we have before our eye that fair consummation, and follow the steps in which he traced out the way to it, we shall do something towards bringing it nearer. With this end

we must begin by striving earnestly ourselves to advance
in that direction. We must seek to obtain the loving
frame of mind, and the happy power of work, which goes
along with it. This must come from a living consciousness
of that infinite Life of nature in which all share, and in
connection with which we are to view first ourselves, but
also all existing things. In this endeavour, we shall cease
to be tormented by the fear of death, because we shall
form the habit of not attaching ourselves too closely in
our acts and thoughts to our own personal and temporal
existence. We shall learn not to separate in thought
our fleeting personal life and activity from the infinite
one, in which we have a share; and not to give ear to our
passionate personal impressions, but only to that higher
insight which we have attained through the ennobling
development of our intellectual and moral powers. The
common opinion, the uncultivated imagination of the
people, which is not enlightened by reason but clouded
over by faith, leads, as Spinoza is ready to allow, to a
different conclusion. It regards each man as free only so
far as he may follow his unreasoning desires, and useful
in so far as he directs himself, in accordance with the
moral law to which salvation is attached. It regards
righteousness and virtue as a burden which is to be laid
down after death, and in place of which man is to receive
his reward for consenting, as a slave, to bear this burden.
It considers that, besides the hope of that reward, there is
no motive but fear of cruel punishment after death that
could induce a man to live according to the law of reason,
so far as the weakness and inability of his nature allow
him to do so; and that, but for these considerations, a
man might fairly give ear to his unreasoning desires, and
neglect his better self entirely. This, Spinoza declared,

was not less absurd than if a man, fearing he should not
be able to feed his body with sound food to all eternity,
should begin at once to treat himself with poisons ; or if,
because he did not consider his soul immortal, he should
begin to live unspiritually and irrationally. "No," he
exclaims in noble indignation, "the life of man is not a
service for wages : what is called happiness is not the
reward of virtue, but virtue itself. We do not enjoy
happiness or virtue, because we are able to govern our
passions ; but we have power to bridle our passions,
because we are rich in happiness and virtue. The way to
reach this end appears to many to be laborious and
difficult; but if happiness lay ready to our hand, and were
to be obtained without exertion, how is it so neglected
by nearly every one ? All that is excellent is difficult and
rare."

It is, however, the great distinction of man, that by
following the lines of his nature he can reach excellence.
There can be no stranger misunderstanding than that of
the false interpretation of Darwinism, which, starting
from man's relation to the brutes, would confine him
within the limits of brute-nature. Not the point from
which any being sprang, but the point to which it has
the capacity to rise, determines the value of its nature ;
and a being descends in the scale in proportion as it
stops short of the goal that is fixed for it, and to its own
misfortune, degenerates from the higher capacity with
which nature endowed it. Man, regarded as belonging
to the animal kingdom, is capable of rising to the highest
nobility ; and the call is addressed to him never to lose
sight of this goal, but always to bring himself and others
nearer to it. The way he has to follow in such an
endeavour was smoothed for him by the thinker, whose

statue we are now about to unveil. In his own life, so
wise and noble, as well as so simple and retiring, he
gave the most attractive picture of the salutary practice
of his doctrine, and showed how to avoid all emotions
which proceed from hatred and anger, and to put away
all narrowness of spirit as unworthy of a reasonable man.
" A bad Jew, and no better Christian," he was called by
Stoupe, the Swiss colonel in the French service, who had
just spoken to him at Utrecht. The author of the phrase
did not imagine that it might contain the highest praise,
as applied to one who was in fact a *man*, raised far above
the partisanship of either of these faiths. May it come
to pass from this time forward, that Jew and Christian
may shake off their prejudices and superstitions of race
and creed, and in his spirit, in accordance with his
principles, grow up to the nobleness of men, cultivated
and full-grown men, persuaded of the reasonableness of
their nature, and of their high calling as moral beings,
and inspired with the most cheerful and happy energy !

And now let the statue be unveiled before us which
the artist-hand of Frederic Hexamer has wrought to be
erected to his memory, to call before us in a worthy
manner his bodily form. Convinced of the reasonable
principle that a slovenly and neglected outer man testifies
rather against any individual than in his favour, he was
accustomed to dress himself carefully when he went out,
and he is, therefore, to appear well-attired in the eyes of
posterity. True, we cannot add to this appearance the
genial address, which when he was alive was wont to add
in a marked degree to the attractiveness of his person ;
yet the artist has taken care that he who gazes on this
bronze image shall find the *man* brought unmistakably
before him, who—in his modest lodging overlooking this

quiet water—wrote down for us such life-awakening thoughts. Our hearty and united thanks are due to him for what he has achieved! And as he has acquitted himself excellently in the task entrusted to his hands, I turn with the more confidence to you, most worthy and honourable Head of this community, to hand over this work to your full and free possession. Accept it as the image of the good spirit of your town—the spirit of most loving wisdom, and most happy and beneficent activity! Fortunate community, who have long seen within your walls the pedestrian and the equestrian statue of that noble beggar-prince and insurgent, which does not cease to speak to you of independent public spirit and united patriotism! and now, see added to these the statue of the sage, who preaches to you the message of human culture, and of elevation above all narrow religious partisanship and social prejudice. The cities of the Middle Ages had their distinctive marks, their pillars of Roland, and things of that sort; but what are they, in comparison with memorials like these! Happy, therefore, the land and people to whom these images, set up in the midst of this community, cease not to speak. Under this prince, the little country of the Netherlands became, three centuries ago, a pattern to Europe, advancing first upon the path of popular freedom in Church and State. May the same country, following the leadership of this philosopher, become no less a guide in the elevation of the intellect and character! In this way it may give a fresh and eloquent testimony to the fact, that—for lands and peoples, as for individuals—moral strength and greatness do not follow the proportions of material things, nor depend on them for the happy exercise of their activity.

IV.

SPINOZA: 1677, AND 1877.

ADDRESS

DELIVERED AT THE UNVEILING OF THE MONUMENT AT
THE HAGUE ON 21st FEBRUARY, 1877.

BY

ERNEST RENAN.

10

SPINOZA: 1677, AND 1877.

ADDRESS

Delivered at the Unveiling of the Monument at the Hague on 21st February, 1877.

On this day two hundred years, in the afternoon, and at about this same hour, there lay dying at the age of forty-three, on the quiet quay of the Pavilioengragt a few paces hence, a poor man, whose life had been so profoundly silent that his last sigh was scarcely heard. He had occupied a retired room in the house of a worthy pair, who, without understanding him, felt for him an instinctive veneration. On the morning of his last day he had gone down as usual to join his hosts; there had been religious services that morning; the gentle philosopher conversed with the good folk about what the minister had said, much approved it, and advised them to conform themselves thereto. The host and hostess (let us name them, their honest sincerity entitles them to a place in this beautiful Idyl of the Hague related by Colerus), the Van der Spycks, husband and wife, went back to their devotions. On their return home, their peaceful lodger was dead. The funeral on the 25th of February was conducted like that of a Christian believer in the new church on the Spuy. All the inhabitants of the district greatly regretted the disappearance of the sage who had lived amongst them as one of themselves.

.10 *

His hosts preserved his memory like a religion, and none who had approached him ever spoke of him without calling him, according to custom, "the blessed Spinoza."

About the same time, however, any one able to track the current of opinion setting in among the professedly enlightened circles of the Pharisaism of that day, would have seen, in singular contrast, the much-loved philosopher of the simple and single-hearted become the bugbear of the narrow orthodoxy which pretended to a monopoly of the truth.   A wretch, a pestilence, an imp of hell, the most wicked atheist that ever lived, a man steeped in crime—this was what the solitary of the Pavilioengragt grew to be in the opinion of right-thinking theologians and philosophers !

Portraits were spread abroad exhibiting him as "bearing on his face the signs of reprobation." A distinguished philosopher—bold as he, but less consistent and less completely sincere—called him "a wretch." But justice was to have her day. The human mind, attaining, in Germany especially, towards the end of the eighteenth century to a more enlightened theology and a wider philosophy, recognized in Spinoza the precursor of a new gospel. Jacobi took the public into his confidence as to a conversation he had held with Lessing. He had gone to Lessing in hopes of enlisting his aid against Spinoza. What was his astonishment on finding in Lessing an avowed Spinozist ! Ἐν καὶ πᾶν, said Lessing to him— this is the whole of philosophy. Him whom a whole century had declared an atheist, Novalis pronounced a "God intoxicated man." His forgotten works were published, and eagerly sought after. Schleiermacher, Goethe, Hegel, Schelling, all with one voice proclaim Spinoza the father of modern thought. Perhaps there may have been some exaggeration in this first outburst of tardy reparation; but time, which sets everything in its place, has substantially ratified Lessing's judgment, and in the present day there is no enlightened mind that does not acknowledge Spinoza as the man who possessed the highest God-consciousness of his day. It is this conviction that has made you decree that his pure and lowly tomb should have its anniversary. It is the common assertion of a free faith in the Infinite, that on this day gathers together, in the spot that witnessed so much virtue, the most select assembly that a man of genius could group round him after his death. A sovereign, as distinguished by intellectual as by moral gifts, is among us in spirit. A prince who can justly appreciate merit of every kind, by distinguishing this solemnity with his presence, desires to testify that of the glories of Holland not one is alien to him, and that no lofty thinking escapes his enlightened judgment, and his philosophic admiration.

I.

The illustrious Baruch de Spinoza was born at Amsterdam, at the time when your Republic was attaining its highest degree of glory and power. He belonged to that great race, which, by the influence it has exerted and the services it has rendered, occupies so exceptional a place in the history of civilization. Miraculous in its own way, the development of the Jewish people ranks side by side with that other miracle, the development of the Greek mind; for, if Greece, from the first realized the ideal of poetry, of science, of philosophy, of art, of profane life, the Jewish people, if I may so speak, has made the religion of humanity. Its prophets inaugurated

in the world the idea of righteousness, the revindication
of the rights of the weak—a revindication so much the
more violent that, all idea of future recompense being
unknown to them, they dreamed of the realization of the
ideal upon this earth and at no distant period.   It was a
Jew, Isaiah, who, seven hundred and fifty years before
Jesus Christ, dared affirm that sacrifices are of little
importance, and that one thing only is needful, purity of
heart and hands.   Then, when earthly events seemed
irremediably to contradict such bright Utopias, Israel can
change front in a way unparalleled.

Transporting into the domain of pure idealism that
kingdom of God with which earth proves incompatible,
one moiety of its children founds Christianity, the other
carries on, through the tortures of the Middle Ages, that
imperturbable protest : " Hear, O Israel, the Lord thy
God is one ; holy is His name." This potent tradition of
idealism, and hope against all hope—this religion, able to
obtain from its adherents the most heroic sacrifices,
though it be not of its essence to promise them any
certainty beyond this life—this was the healthy and
bracing medium in which Spinoza developed himself.
His education was at first entirely Hebraic; the great
literature of Israel was his earliest, and, in point of fact,
his perpetual instructress—was the meditation of all his
life.

As generally happens, Hebrew literature, in assuming
the character of a sacred book, had become the subject
of a conventional exegesis, much less intent upon
explaining the old texts according to the meaning in
their authors' minds than on finding in them aliment for
the moral and religious wants of the day.   The penetrating mind of the young Spinoza soon discerned all the

defects of the exegesis of the Synagogue; the Bible, as
taught him, was disfigured by the accumulated per-
versions of more than two thousand years. He determined
to pierce beyond these. He was, indeed, essentially at
one with the true fathers of Judaism, and especially with
that great Maimonides who found a way of introducing
into Judaism the most daring speculations of philosophy.
He foresaw, with wondrous sagacity, the great results of
the critical exegesis, destined a hundred and twenty-five
years later to afford the true meaning of the noblest
productions of Hebrew genius. Was this to destroy the
Bible? Has that admirable literature lost by being
understood in its real aspect, rather than relegated outside of the common laws of humanity? Certainly not.
The truths revealed by science invariably surpass the
dreams that science dispels. The world of Laplace
exceeds in beauty, I imagine, that of a Cosmas
Indicopleustes, who pictured the universe to himself as a
casket, on the lid of which the stars glide along in grooves
at a few leagues from us. In the same way the Bible is
more beautiful when we have learnt to see therein—
ranged in order on a canvas of a thousand years—each
aspiration, each sigh, each prayer of the most exalted
religious consciousness that ever existed, then when we
force ourselves to view it as a book unlike any other,
composed, preserved, interpreted in direct opposition to
all the ordinary rules of the human intellect.

But the persecutions of the Middle Ages had produced
on Judaism the usual effect of all persecution; they
had rendered minds narrow and timid. A few years
previously, at Amsterdam, the unfortunate Uriel Acosta
had cruelly expiated certain doubts that fanaticism finds
as culpable as avowed incredulity. The boldness of the

young Spinoza was still worse received ; he was anathe-
matized, and had to submit to an excommunication that
he had not courted. A very old history this ! Religious
communions, beneficent cradles of so much earnestness
and so much virtue, do not allow of any refusal to be
shut up exclusively within their embrace ; they claim to
imprison for ever the life that had its beginnings within
them ; they brand as apostasy the lawful emancipation of
the mind that seeks to take its flight alone. It is as
though the egg should reproach, as ungrateful, the bird
that had escaped therefrom : the egg was necessary in its
time,—when it became a bondage it had to be broken.
A great marvel truly that Erasmus of Rotterdam should
feel himself cramped in his cell, that Luther should not
prefer his monkish vows to that far holier vow which
man by the very fact of his being contracts with truth.
Had Erasmus persisted in his monastic routine, or
Luther gone on distributing indulgences, they would
have been apostates indeed. Spinoza was the greatest
of modern Jews, and Judaism exiled him : nothing more
simple ; it must have been so; it must be so ever. Finite
symbols, prisons of the infinite spirit, will eternally
protest against the effort of Idealism to enlarge them.
The spirit on its side struggles eternally for more air and
more light. Eighteen hundred and fifty years ago the
Synagogue denounced as a seducer the one who was to
raise the maxims of the Synagogue to unequalled glory.
And the Christian Church, how often has she not driven
from her breast those who should have been her chiefest
honour ! In cases like these our duty is fulfilled if we
retain a pious memory of the education our childhood
received. Let the old Churches be free to brand with
criminality those who quit them ; they shall not succeed

in obtaining from us any but grateful feelings, since, after all, the harm they are able to do us is as nothing compared to the good they have done.

II.

Here then we have the excommunicated of the Synagogue of Amsterdam forced to create for himself a spiritual abode outside of the home which rejected him. He had great sympathy with Christianity, but he dreaded all chains,—he did not embrace it. Descartes had just renewed philosophy by his firm and sober rationalism. Descartes was his master; Spinoza took up the problems where they had been left by that great mind, but saw that through fear of the Sorbonne his theology had always remained somewhat arid. Oldenburg asking him one day what fault he could find with the philosophy of Descartes and of Bacon, Spinoza replied that their chief fault lay in not sufficiently occupying themselves with the First Cause. Perhaps his reminiscences of Jewish theology, that ancient wisdom of the Hebrews before which he often bows, suggested to him higher views, and more sublime aspirations in this matter. Not only the ideas held by the vulgar, but those even of thinkers on Divinity, appeared to him inadequate. He saw plainly that there is no assigning a limited part to the Infinite, that Divinity is all, or is nothing; that if the Divine be a reality it must pervade all. For twenty years he meditated on these problems without for a moment averting his thoughts. Our distaste nowadays for system and abstract formula no longer permits us to accept absolutely the propositions within which he had thought to confine the secrets of the Infinite. For Spinoza, as for Descartes, the universe was only extension and thought; chemistry and physiology were lacking to that great school, which was too exclusively geometrical and mechanical. A stranger to the idea of life, and those notions as to the constitution of bodies that chemistry was destined to reveal—too much attached still to the scholastic expressions of substance and attribute—Spinoza did not attain to that living and fertile Infinite, shown us by the science of nature and of history, as presiding in space unbounded, over a development more and more intense; but, making allowance for a certain dryness in expression, what grandeur there is in that inflexible geometrical deduction, leading up to the supreme proposition: "It is of the nature of the Substance to develop itself necessarily by an infinity of infinite attributes infinitely modified!" God is thus absolute thought, universal consciousness. The ideal exists, nay, it is the true existence; all else is mere appearance and frivolity. Bodies and souls are mere modes of which God is the substance: it is only the modes that fall within duration, the substance is all in eternity. Thus, God does not prove Himself, His existence results from His sole idea; everything supposes and contains Him. God is the condition of all existence, all thought. If God did not exist, thought would be able to conceive more than nature could furnish, which is a contradiction.

Spinoza did not clearly discern universal progress; the world, as he conceives it, seems as if it were crystallized in a matter which is incorruptible extension, in a soul that is immutable thought; the sentiment of God deprives him of the sentiment of man; for ever face to face with the Infinite, he did not sufficiently perceive what of the Divine conceals itself in relative manifestations; but he, better than any other, saw the eternal identity which constitutes the basis of all transitory evolutions. Whatever is limited seems to him frivolous and unworthy to occupy a philosopher. Bold in flight, he soared straight to the lofty snow-covered summits, without casting a glance on the rich display of life springing up on the mountain's side. _ At an altitude where every breast but his own pants hard, he lives, he enjoys, he flourishes there as men in general do in mild and temperate regions. What he for his part needs is the glacier air, keen and penetrating. He does not ask to be followed. He is like Moses, to whom secrets unknown to the crowd reveal themselves on the heights; but be sure of this—he was the seer of his age, he was in his own day the one who saw deepest into God.

III.

It might have been supposed that, all alone on these snowy peaks, he would turn out in human affairs wrong-headed, utopian, or scornfully sceptical. Nothing of the kind. He was incessantly occupied with the application of his principles to human society. The pessimism of Hobbes, and the dreams of Thomas More were equally repugnant to him. One half at least of the *Theologico-Political Treatise* which appeared in 1670, might be reprinted to-day without losing any of its appropriateness. Listen to its admirable title:—"Tractatus Theologico-Politicus, continens dissertationes aliquot, quibus ostenditur, libertatem philosophandi non tantum salva pietate et reipublicæ pace posse concedi, sed eamdem nisi cum pace reipublicæ ipsaque pietate tolli non posse." For centuries past it has been supposed that society rested on metaphysical dogmas. Spinoza discerns profoundly that these dogmas, assumed to be necessary to humanity, yet cannot escape discussion; that revelation itself—if there be one—traversing, in order to reach us, the faculties of the human mind, is no less than all else amendable to criticism. I wish I could quote in its entirety that admirable Chapter XX, in which our great publicist establishes with masterly skill that dogma—new then, and still contested in our own day—which styles itself liberty of conscience.

"The final end of the State," he says, "consists not in dominating over men, restraining them by fears, subjecting them to the will of others, but, on the contrary, in permitting each one to live in all possible security; that is to say, in preserving intact the natural right of each to live without injury to himself or others. No, I say, the State has not for its end the transformation of men from reasonable beings into animals or automata; it has for end so to act that its citizens should in security develop soul and body, and make free use of their reason. Hence the true end of the State is liberty. Whosoever means to respect the rights of a sovereign should never act in opposition to his decrees; but each has the right to think what he will, and to say what he thinks, provided he content himself with speaking and teaching in the name of pure reason, and do not attempt on his private authority to introduce innovations into the State. For example, a citizen who demonstrates that a certain law is repugnant to sound reason, and holds that for that cause it ought to be abrogated—if he submit his opinions to the judgment of the sovereign, to whom alone it belongs to establish and to abolish laws, and if meanwhile he acts in no wise contrary to law—that man certainly deserves well of the State as the best of citizens. . . .

"Even if we admit the possibility of so stifling men's liberty, and laying such a yoke upon them that they dare not even whisper without the approbation of the sovereign, never most surely can they be prevented from thinking as they will. What then must ensue? That men will think one way and speak another; that consequently good faith—a virtue most necessary to the State— will become corrupted; that adulation—a detestable thing—and perfidy will be had in repute, entailing the decadence of all good and healthy morality. What can be more disastrous to a State than to exile honest citizens as evil-doers, because they do not share the opinions of the crowd, and are ignorant of the art of feigning? What more fatal than to treat as enemies and doom to death men whose only crime is that of thinking independently? The scaffold, which should be the terror of the wicked, is thus turned into the glorious theatre where virtue and toleration shine out in all their lustre, and publicly cover the sovereign majesty with approbrium. Beyond question there is only one thing to be learnt from such a spectacle—to imitate those noble martyrs : or, if one fears death, to become the cowardly flatterers of power. Nothing, then, is so full of peril as to refer, and submit to divine rights, matters of pure speculation, and to impose laws on opinions which are, or may be, subjects of discussion among men. If the authority of the State limited itself to the repression of actions, while allowing impunity to words, controversies would less often turn into seditions."

More sagacious than many so-called practical men, our speculator sees perfectly well that the only durable Governments are the reasonable, and that the only reasonable Governments are the constitutional. Far from absorbing the individual in the State, he gives him solid guarantees against the State's omnipotence. He is no revolutionary, but a moderate ; he transforms, explains, but does not destroy. His God is not indeed one who takes pleasure in ceremonies, sacrifices, odour of incense, yet Spinoza has no design whatever to overthrow religion. He entertains a profound veneration for Christianity, a tender and a sincere respect. The supernatural, however, has no meaning in his doctrine. According to his principles, anything out of nature would be out of being, and therefore inconceivable. Prophets, revealers, have been men like others :—

"It is not thinking but dreaming," he says, "to hold that prophets have had a human body and not a human soul, and that consequently their knowledge and their sensations have been of a different nature from ours." " The prophetic faculty has not been the dowry of one people only, the Jewish people. The quality of Son of God has not been the privilege of one man only. . . . To

state my views openly, I tell you that it is not absolutely necessary
to know Christ after the flesh ; but it is otherwise when we speak
of that Son of God, that is to say, that eternal Wisdom of God,
which has manifested itself in all things, and more fully in the
human soul, and above all in Jesus Christ. Without this wisdom
no one can attain the state of beautitude, since it alone teaches us
what is true and what is false, what is right and what is wrong.
. . . As to what certain Churches have added, . . . I have
expressly warned you that I do not know what they mean, and to
speak frankly I may confess that they seem to me to be using the
same sort of language as if they spoke of a circle assuming the
nature of a square."

Was not this exactly what Schleiermacher said ? and
as to Spinoza, the fellow-founder with Richard Simon of
Biblical exegesis, was not he the precursor of those
liberal theologians who have in our own day shown that
Christianity can retain all its glory without super-
naturalism ? His letters to Oldenburg on the resurrection
of Jesus Christ, and of the manner in which St. Paul
understood it, are masterpieces which a hundred years
later would have served as the manifesto of a whole school
of critical theology.

In the eyes of Spinoza it signifies little whether
mysteries be understood this way or that, provided they
be understood in a pious sense. Religion has one aim
only, piety ; and we are to appeal to it, not for metaphysics,
but for practical guidance. At bottom there is but one
single thing in Scripture as in all revelation : " Love your
neighbour." The fruit of religion is blessedness ; each
one participating in it according to his capacity and his
efforts. The souls that are governed by reason—the
philosophic souls that have even in this world their life in
God—are safe from death ; what death takes from them
is of no value ; but weak or passionate souls perish almost
entirely, and death, instead of being for them a simple

accident, involves the foundation of their being. . . . The ignorant man, who lets himself be swayed by blind passions, is agitated in a thousand different directions by external causes, and never enjoys true peace of soul; for him ceasing to suffer means ceasing to be. The soul of the wise man, on the other hand, can scarcely be troubled. Possessing by a kind of eternal necessity the conscious-ness of itself and of God and of things, he never ceases to be, and ever preserves the soul's true peace.

Spinoza could not endure his system to be considered irreligious or subversive. The timid Oldenburg did not conceal from him that some of his opinions seemed to certain readers to tend to the overthrow of piety. "Whatever accords with reason," replied Spinoza, "is in my belief most favourable to the practice of virtue." The pretended superiority of coarsely positive concep-tions as to religion and a future life found him intractable. "Is it, I ask, to cast off religion," he was wont to say, "to acknowledge God as the Supreme Good, and thence to conclude that he must be loved with a free soul? To maintain that all our felicity and most perfect freedom consists in that love—that the reward of virtue is virtue, and that a blind and impotent soul finds its punishment in its blindness—is this a denial of all religion?" At the root of all such attacks he traced meanness of soul. According to him any one who felt irritated by a disin-terested religion involuntarily confessed reason and virtue to have no charm in his eyes, and that his pleasure would lie in living to indulge his passions if he were not restrained by fear. "Thus then," he would add, "such a one only abstains from evil and obeys the Divine com-mandment regretfully as a slave, and in return for this slavery expects from God rewards which have infinitely

more value in his eyes than the Divine law. The more
aversion and estrangement from good he may have felt,
the more he hopes to be recompensed, and imagines that
they who are not restrained by the same fear as himself
do what he would do in their case—that is to say, live
lawlessly." Spinoza held with reason that this manner
of seeking heaven was contrary to reason, and that there
is an absurdity in pretending to gain God's favour by
owning to him that, did one not dread him, one would
not love.

IV.

He was, however, well aware of the danger of inter-
fering with beliefs, in which few admit these subtle
distinctions. *Cauté* was his motto, and, his friends
having made him aware of the explosion that the *Ethica*
would infallibly produce, he kept it unpublished till his
death. He had no literary vanity, nor did he seek cele-
brity—possibly, indeed, because he was sure to obtain it
without seeking. He was perfectly happy. He has told
us so—let us take him at his word. He has done still
better; he has bequeathed us his secret. Let all men
listen to the recipe of the "Prince of Atheists" for the
discovery of happiness—it is the love of God. To love
God is to live in God. Life in God is the best and most
perfect because it is the reasonablest, happiest, fullest—
in a word, because it gives us more *being* than any other
life, and satisfies most completely the fundamental desire
that constitutes our essence.

Spinoza's whole practical life was regulated according
to these maxims. That life was a masterpiece of good
sense and judgment. It was led with the profound skill
of the wise man who desires one thing only, and inva-

riably ends by obtaining it. Never did policy so well combine means and end. Had he been less reticent, he would perhaps have met the same fate as the unfortunate Acosta. Loving truth for its own sake, he was indifferent to the abuse that his constancy in speaking it entailed, and answered never a word to the attacks made on him. For his part he attacked no one. " It is foreign to my habits," he said, " to look out for the errors into which authors have fallen." Had he desired to be an official personage, his life would no doubt have been traversed by persecution, or at least by disgrace. He was nothing, and desired to be nothing. *Ama nesciri* was his desire, as well as that of the author of the *De Imitatione.* He sacrificed everything to peace of mind; and, in so doing, there was no selfishness, for his mind was of importance to the world. He frequently refused wealth on its way to him, and desired only what was absolutely necessary. The King of France offered him a pension; he declined. The Elector Palatine offered him a chair at Heidelberg : " Your freedom shall be complete," he was told, " for the prince is convinced that you will not abuse it to disturb the established religion." " I do not very well understand," he replied, " within what limits it would be necessary to confine that philosophical freedom granted me on condition of not disturbing the established religion; and then again, the instruction I bestowed on youth would interfere with my own advance in philosophy. I have only succeeded in procuring for myself a tranquil life by the renunciation of all kinds of public teaching." He felt that his duty was to think. He thought, in fact, for humanity, whose ideas he forestalled by more than two centuries.

The same instinctive sagacity was carried by him into

11

all the relations of life; he felt that public opinion never
permits a man to be daring in two directions at once;
being a free-thinker, he looked upon himself as bound to
live like a saint. But I am wrong in saying this; was
not this pure and gentle life rather the direct expression
of his peaceful and lovable consciousness? At that
period the Atheist was pictured as a villain armed with
daggers. Spinoza was throughout his whole lifetime
humble, meek, pious. His enemies were ingenuous
enough to object to this: they would have liked him to
live conformably to the conventional type, and, after the
career of a demon incarnate, to die in despair. Spinoza
smiled at this singular pretension, and refused to oblige
his enemies by changing his way of life. He had warm
friends, he showed himself courageous at need, he pro-
tested against popular indignation wherever he thought
it unjust. Many disappointments failed to shake his
fidelity to the Republican party; the liberality of his
opinions was never at the mercy of events. What perhaps does him more honour still, he possessed the esteem
and sincere affection of the simple beings among whom
he lived. Nothing is equal in value to the esteem of the
lowly; their judgment is almost always that of God.
To the worthy Van der Spycks, he was evidently the
very ideal of a perfect lodger. " No one ever gave less
trouble," was their testimony given some years after his
death to Colerus. "While in the house he inconvenienced
nobody; he spent the best part of his time quietly in
his own room. If he chanced to tire himself by too
protracted meditation, he would come down stairs and
speak to the family about any subject of common talk,
even about trifles." In fact, there could never have
been a more affable inmate. He would often hold

conversations with his hostess, especially at the time of her confinements, as well as with the rest of the household when any sorrow or sickness befell them. He would tell the children to go to divine service, and when they returned from the sermon ask them how much they remembered of it. He almost always strongly seconded what the preacher had said. One of the persons he most esteemed was the Pastor Cordes, an excellent man and good expounder of the Scriptures : sometimes, indeed, he went to hear him, and he advised his host never to miss the preaching of so able a man. One day his hostess asked him if he thought she could be saved in the religion she professed : "Your religion is a good one," he replied, "you should not seek any other, nor doubt that yours will procure salvation if in attaching yourself to piety you lead at the same time a peaceful and tranquil life."

His temperance and good management were admirable. His daily wants were provided for by a handicraft in which he became very skilful—the polishing of lenses. The Van der Spycks made over to Colerus scraps of paper, on which Spinoza had noted down his expenses ; these averaged about fourpence halfpenny a day. He was very careful to settle his accounts every quarter, so as neither to spend more nor less than his income. He dressed simply, if not poorly, but his aspect radiated serenity. It was evident that he had found out a doctrine which gave him perfect content.

He was never elated, and never depressed; the equability of his moods seems wonderful. Perhaps, indeed, he may have felt some sadness when the daughter of his Professor, Van den Ende, preferred Kerkering to him ; but I suspect that he soon consoled himself.

" Reason is my enjoyment," he would say, "and the aim I have in this life is joy and serenity." He objected to any praise of sadness :—

"It is superstition," he maintained, "that sets up sadness as good, and all that tends to joy as evil. God would show himself envious if He took pleasure in my impotence, and in the ills I suffer. Rather in proportion to the greatness of our joy do we attain to a greater perfection, and participate more fully in the divine nature. . . . Joy, therefore, can never be evil so long as it be regulated by the law of our true utility. A virtuous life is not a sad and sombre one, a life of privations and austerity. How should the Divinity take pleasure in the spectacle of my weakness, or impute to me, as meritorious, tears, sobs, terrors—signs all of an impotent soul? Yes," he added emphatically, "it is the part of a wise man to use the things of this life, and enjoy them as much as possible; to recruit himself by a temperate and appetizing diet; to charm his senses with the perfume and the brilliant verdure of plants; to adorn his very attire, to enjoy music, games, spectacles, and every diversion that any one can bestow on himself, without detriment to character." "We are, incessantly spoken to of repentance, humility, death; but repentance is not a virtue, but the consequence of a weakness. Nor is humility one, since it springs in man from the idea of his inferiority. As to the thought of death, it is the daughter of fear, and it is in feeble souls that it sets up its home." "The thing of all others," he would say, "about which a free man thinks least is death. Wisdom lies in the contemplation not of death but of life."

V.

Since the days of Epictetus and Marcus Aurelius, no life had been witnessed so profoundly penetrated by the sentiment of the Divine. In the twelfth, thirteenth, and sixteenth century, rationalistic philosophy had numbered very great men in its ranks, but it had had no saints. Occasionally a very repulsive and hard element had entered into the finest characters amongst Italian free-thinkers. Religion had been utterly absent from those lives not less in revolt against human than divine laws, of which the last example was that of poor Vanini. Here, on the contrary, we have religion producing freethought as a part of piety. Religion in a system such as this is not a portion of life, it is life itself. That which is seen to matter here is not the being in possession of some metaphysical phrases more or less correct, it is the giving to one's life a sure pole, a supreme direction—the ideal.

It is by so doing that your illustrious countryman has lifted up a banner, which still avails to shelter beneath it all who think and feel nobly. Yes, religion is eternal; it answers to the first need of primitive, as well as of civilized man; it will only perish with humanity itself, or, rather, its disappearance would be the proof that degenerate humanity was about to re-enter the mere animalism out of which it had emerged. And yet no dogma, no worship, no formula, can in these days of ours exhaust the religious sentiment. We must confront with each other these seemingly contradictory assertions. Woe to him who pretends that the era of religions is past! Woe to him who imagines it possible to restore to the old symbols the force they had when they leant upon the imperturbable dogmatism of other days! With that dogmatism we, for our part, must needs dispense; we must dispense with those fixed creeds, sources of so many struggles and divisions, but sources no less of such fervent convictions; we must give up believing that it is our part to hold down others in a faith we no longer share. Spinoza was right in his horror of hypocrisy. Hypocrisy is cowardly and dishonest, but, above all, hypocrisy is useless. Who is it, indeed, that is deceived here? The persistency of the higher classes in un-

qualifiedly patronizing, in sight of the uncultivated
classes, the religious reforms of other days will have but
one effect—that of impairing their own authority at
those times of crisis, when it is important that the
people should still believe in the reason and the virtue of
a few.

Honour then to Spinoza who has dared to say : Reason
before all ; reason can never be contrary to the well-
understood interests of humanity.   But we would remind
those who are carried away by unreflecting impatience
that Spinoza never conceived of religious revolution as
being aught else than a transformation of formulas.
According to him what was fundamental went on sub-
sisting under other terms. If he on one hand energetically
repudiated the theocratic power of the clergy, as distinguished from civil society, or the tendency of the
State to occupy itself with metaphysics, on the other
hand he never denied either the State or religion.   He
wished the State tolerant and religion free.   We wish for
nothing more.   One cannot impose on others beliefs one
does not possess.   That the believers of other days made
themselves persecutors proved them tyrannical, but at
least consistent ; as for us, if we were to act as they did,
we should be simply absurd.   Our religion is a sentiment
capable of clothing itself in numerous forms.   These
forms are free from being equally good ; but not one of
them has strength or authority to expel all others.
Freedom—this is the last word of Spinoza's religious
policy.   Let it be the last word of ours !   It is the most
honest course ; it may, perhaps, also be the most
efficacious and certain of the progress of civilization.

Humanity, indeed, advances on the way of progress by
prodigiously unequal steps.   The rude and violent Esau

is out of patience with the slow pace of Jacob's flock.
Let us give time to all. We may not, indeed, permit
simplicity and ignorance to hinder the free movements of
the intellect, but let us not either interfere with the slow
evolution of less active intelligences. The liberty of
absurdity in these is the condition of the liberty of reason
in those. Services rendered to the human mind by
violence are not services after all. That such as lay no
stress on truth should exercise constraint in order to
obtain outward submission, what can be more natural?
But we, who believe that truth is something real, and
deserving of supreme respect, how can we dream of
obtaining by force an adherence, which is valueless except
as the fruit of free conviction? We no longer admit
sacramental formulas, operating by their own virtue,
independently of the mind of him to whom they are
applied. In our eyes a belief has no worth if it be not
gained by the reflection of the individual, if he have
not understood and assimilated it. A mental conviction
brought about by superior order is as absolute nonsense
as love obtained by force or sympathy by command. Let
us promise to ourselves not only to defend our own
liberty against all who seek to attack it, but, if need be,
to defend the liberty of those who have not always
respected ours, and who, it is probable, if they were the
masters, would not respect it.

It is Holland that had the glory, more than two
hundred years ago, to demonstrate the possibility of
these theories by realizing them.

" Must we prove," said Spinoza, " that this freedom of thought
gives rise to no serious inconvenience, and that it is competent to
keep men, openly diverse in their opinions, reciprocally respectful
of each other's rights? Examples abound, nor need we go far to

seek them; let us instance the town of Amsterdam, whose considerable growth—an object of admiration to other nations—is
simply the fruit of this freedom.   In the midst of this flourishing
Republic, this eminent city, men of all nations and all sects live
together in most perfect concord; . . . and there is no sect,
however odious, whose adepts, provided they do not offend against
the rights of any, may not meet with public aid and protection
before the magistrates."

Descartes was of the same opinion when he came to
ask from this country the calm essential to his thinking.
Later, thanks to that noble privilege of a free land
so gloriously maintained by your fathers against all
opponents, your Holland became the asylum where the
human intellect, sheltered from the tyrannies that over-
spread Europe, found air to breathe, a public to comprehend it, organs to multiply its voice then gagged
elsewhere.

Deep assuredly are the wounds of our age, and cruel
are its perplexities.   It can never be with impunity that
so many problems present themselves all at once before
the elements for solving them are in our possession.   It
is not we who have shattered that paradise of crystal,
with its silver and azure gleams, by which so many eyes
have been ravished and consoled.   But there it is in
fragments. What is shattered is shattered, and never will
an earnest spirit undertake the puerile task of bringing
back ignorance destroyed, or restoring illusions dispelled.
The populations of great towns have almost everywhere
lost faith in the supernatural; were we to sacrifice our
convictions and our sincerity in an attempt to give it
them back, we should not succeed.   But the supernatural as formerly understood is not the ideal.

The cause of the supernatural is compromised, the
cause of the ideal is untouched.   It ever will be so.   The

ideal remains the soul of the world, the permanent God, the primordial, efficient, and final Cause of this universe. This it the basis of eternal religion. We, no more than Spinoza, need, in order to adore God, miracles or self-interested prayers. So long as there be in the human heart one fibre to vibrate at the sound of what is true, just, and honest, so long as the instinctively pure prefer purity to life, so long as there be found friends of truth ready to sacrifice their repose to science, friends of goodness to devote themselves to useful and holy works of mercy; woman-hearts to love whatever is worthy, beautiful, and pure; artists to render it by sound, and colour, and inspired accents—so long will God live in us. It could only be when egoism, meanness of soul, narrowness of mind, indifference to knowledge, contempt for human rights, oblivion of what is great and noble, invaded the world—it could only be then that God would cease to be in humanity. But far from us be thoughts like these!

Our aspirations, our sufferings, our very faults and rashness, are the proof that the ideal lives in us. Yes, human life is still something divine! Our apparent negations are often merely the scruples of timid minds that fear to overpass the limits of their knowledge. They are a worthier homage to the Divinity than the hypocritical adoration of a spirit of routine. God is still us, believe it. God is in us! *Est Deus in vobis.*

Let us all unite in bending before the great and illustrious thinker, who two hundred years ago proved better than any other, both by the examples of his life and by the power—still fresh and young—of his works—how much there is of spiritual joy and holy unction in thoughts like these. Let us with Schleiermacher pay the

12

homage of the best we can do to the ashes of the holy and misunderstood Spinoza.

"The sublime spirit of the world penetrated him, the infinite was his beginning and his end; the universal his only and eternal love; living in holy innocence and profound humility, he contemplated himself in the eternal world and saw that he too was for that world a mirror worthy of love; he was full of religion and full of the holy spirit; and therefore he appears to us solitary and unequalled: master in his art, but lifted above the profane, without disciples and without right of citizenship anywhere."

That right of citizenship you are now about to confer on him. Your monument will be the link between his genius and the earth. His spirit will brood like a guardian angel over the spot where his rapid journey among men came to its end. Woe to him who, in passing by, should dare to level an insult at that gentle and pensive figure! He would be punished as all vulgar hearts are punished—by his very vulgarity, and his impotence to comprehend the divine. Spinoza meanwhile from his granite pedestal shall teach to all the way of happiness he himself had found, and for ages to come the cultivated man who passes along the Pavilioengragt will inwardly say, "It is from hence perhaps that God has been seen most near!"

www.ingramcontent.com/pod-product-compliance
Lightning Source LLC
Chambersburg PA
CBHW032011060726
47497CB00017B/2933